W9-CBW-085

"I've stared death in the face more times than I can count. And won.

"I don't know if you know anything about the Cheyenne Dog Soldiers, but they were the cream of the crop among our nation's warriors. My mother's side boasted Dog Soldiers and medicine people. All of the women were warriors by bloodline and tradition."

Jessie leaned closer. "I'm a war woman, Mace. The blood of the Dog Soldiers runs in my veins, and I'm very good at what I do. A soldier's job is to protect the village and the people in it. When it comes down to getting the job done, I don't play around. I'm all business—and I'm not in the business of losing."

Dear Reader,

What's hot this spring? Silhouette Bombshell! We're putting action, danger, romance and that exhilarating feeling of winning against the odds right at your fingertips.

Feeling wild? *USA TODAY* bestselling author Lindsay McKenna's *Wild Woman* takes you to Hong Kong for the latest story in the SISTERS OF THE ARK miniseries. Pilot Jessica "Wild Woman" Merrill is on a mission to infiltrate the lair of a criminal mastermind—but she's been thrown a curveball in the form of an unexpected partner....

The clock is ticking as an NSA code breaker races to stop a bomb in *Countdown* by Ruth Wind, the latest in the high-octane ATHENA FORCE continuity series. This determined Athena woman will risk her career and even kidnap an FBI bomb squad member to save the day!

Indiana Jones and Lara Croft have nothing on modern legend Veronica Bright, the star of author Sharron McClellan's *The Midas Trap*. Veronica has a chance to find the mythical Midas Stone—but to succeed, she's got to risk working for a man who tried to ruin her years ago....

Meet CPA Whitney "Pink" Pearl, heroine of *Show Her the Money* by Stephanie Feagan. Blowing the whistle on a corporate funny-money scam lands her in the red, but Pink won't let death threats, abduction attempts or steamy kisses from untrustworthy lawyers get in the way of justice!

Please send your comments to me c/o Silhouette Books, 233 Broadway, Suite 1001, New York, NY 10279.

Sincerely,

Natashya Wilson

Natashya Wilson
Associate Senior Editor, Silhouette Bombshell

Please address questions and book requests to:
Silhouette Reader Service
U.S.: 3010 Walden Ave., P.O. Box 1325, Buffalo, NY 14269
Canadian: P.O. Box 609, Fort Erie, Ont. L2A 5X3

LINDSAY McKENNA

WILD WOMAN

Published by Silhouette Books

America's Publisher of Contemporary Romance

If you purchased this book without a cover you should be aware that this book is stolen property. It was reported as "unsold and destroyed" to the publisher, and neither the author nor the publisher has received any payment for this "stripped book."

 SILHOUETTE BOOKS

ISBN 0-373-51351-8

WILD WOMAN

Copyright © 2005 by Lindsay McKenna

All rights reserved. Except for use in any review, the reproduction or utilization of this work in whole or in part in any form by any electronic, mechanical or other means, now known or hereafter invented, including xerography, photocopying and recording, or in any information storage or retrieval system, is forbidden without the written permission of the editorial office, Silhouette Books, 233 Broadway, New York, NY 10279 U.S.A.

All characters in this book have no existence outside the imagination of the author and have no relation whatsoever to anyone bearing the same name or names. They are not even distantly inspired by any individual known or unknown to the author, and all incidents are pure invention.

This edition published by arrangement with Harlequin Books S.A.

® and TM are trademarks of Harlequin Books S.A., used under license. Trademarks indicated with ® are registered in the United States Patent and Trademark Office, the Canadian Trade Marks Office and in other countries.

www.SilhouetteBombshell.com

Printed in U.S.A.

Books by Lindsay McKenna

LINDSAY McKENNA

A homeopathic educator, Lindsay teaches at the Desert Institute of Classical Homeopathy in Phoenix, Arizona. When she isn't teaching alternative medicine, she is writing books about love. She feels love is the single greatest healer in the world and hopes that her books touch her readers' hearts.

To a great and dear friend: Cathy Shehorn,
who is learning to be one herself.

Chapter 1

"With all due respect, I *refuse* to be saddled with a woman on this mission." CIA Agent Mace Phillips sat in a chair stubbornly facing Morgan Trayhern, who oversaw Perseus, a supersecret CIA-funded organization, and Trayhern's second-in-command, retired U.S. Army Major Mike Houston. Mace saw Morgan Trayhern's gray eyes narrow speculatively, while amusement glimmered in Houston's eyes.

Tapping his fingers on the bird's-eye maple desk where he was seated, Morgan nodded and said, "I see…." then glanced up at Houston, who stood beside him. "Mike, would you care to tell Agent

Phillips that he's on special assignment from the CIA and, technically, works for us now?"

"Be glad to," Mike replied. "Agent Phillips, we realize that the CIA does things differently than we do at Perseus and Medusa. However, the reason behind our success is simple. We team up a man and a woman on all undercover missions. We know the CIA and FBI don't have this policy. But when we do interface with these agencies, it is understood that the individual working for us plays by our rules." Mike saw Phillips's face become slightly tinged with a flush, his large, wide-set green eyes growing dark and sullen looking as he sat at attention, his hands on his thighs.

"They aren't idle rules, Agent Phillips," Morgan added, his voice smooth and even. He sensed that Phillips, who was dressed in a typical CIA uniform of a dark suit, white shirt and conservative light blue tie, was getting increasingly upset.

"Men have their unique skills, and so do women. Male and female agents, therefore, see and do things a little differently."

"Correct," Houston said, grinning at Morgan before turning his attention back to Mace. "Women perceive things that we men are blind, deaf and dumb to most of the time. That ability to detect the nuances of a case can mean the difference between life and death. Women are our secret weapon at

Perseus and Medusa, Agent Phillips, and we think enough of you to team you up with one."

Mace slid his index finger between his damp neck and the tight collar of his white cotton shirt. He didn't want to be here. In fact, he wanted to run away from this hidden enclave in the small town of Phillipsburg, Montana. Why oh why had he volunteered for this mission?

He knew why. He was bored out of his skull as a Chinese translator these last three months at Langley, Virginia, CIA headquarters. Shoved away in a room to review Chinese satellite transmissions and phone conversations. Typing up unending reports. He hated it. He was a field agent, not some office grunt.

When he'd joined the CIA after being discharged from the Marine Corps as a recon—or reconnaissance—he received training as an undercover operative before serving in the field for five years. Recently, his proficiency with the Mandarin and Cantonese languages had secured him placement in Southeast Asia before being ordered to Langley. When Mace learned that the agency needed an undercover field agent to travel to Hong Kong to locate a stolen artifact, he'd leaped at the assignment to escape the drudgery of his endless translation duties.

Now, he was sorry. "I have nothing against women," he said brusquely. "I've always operated alone in the field."

Morgan opened a file. "From what I can see here, Agent Phillips, you work in intel back in Langley."

"That's correct, sir. But..." He snapped his mouth shut. These men didn't care about his unhappiness at being confined to a sealed room invulnerable to enemy surveillance or eavesdropping. The lead-lined room, which couldn't be bugged, had a dead energy; he felt as if he was walking into a vacuum every morning at work.

Houston cocked his head. "But what, Agent Phillips?"

Squirming inwardly, Mace said through thinned lips, "I can't talk about it."

"There are no secrets, Agent Phillips," Morgan said. "We have Q clearance."

Mace knew that Q clearance was reserved for those at the highest levels of government, the president of the United States being one of them. Feeling a prickle of heat begin at his neck and sweep upward, Mace wished that this adolescent response would end. He was twenty-nine years old, a former marine and a CIA agent, and he was blushing! Grimacing, he muttered, "All right, sir. The 'but' is that I've been stuck in intel for the last three months. I was supposed to be assigned as a field agent in Southeast Asia because of my capabilities in the two main Chinese languages. Instead, I was told to stay at Langley because of my expertise in Chinese translation. I don't care for the job. I need to be out in the field."

Morgan chuckled. "Sticking you in a building to translate is a certifiable waste of your talents, Agent Phillips. You were a recon marine. You're used to action. You know how to think outside the box in a dangerous situation. And you're used to relying on the other members of your team."

Feeling a wave of relief, Mace nodded. He knew Morgan had been a captain in the Marine Corps. The man was a living legend among the U.S. military services. In the closing days of the Vietnam War Morgan's company had been overrun and only he and another man survived. Mace respected Morgan Trayhern. When he'd found out the assignment would mean working with Morgan, he thought he'd died and gone to heaven. Until he learned he had to have a female partner. That part sucked.

"We had twenty-five applications for this mission," Houston added. "We chose *you* because Morgan here knows that marine recons are specially trained for teamwork."

Morgan leaned forward on his elbows to hold Mace's gaze. "Now, Agent Phillips," he said, softening his deep voice slightly, "if you're going to sit there and tell me you positively can't work as a *team* member, then we will have to release you back to Langley."

Picking up a file from the desk, Houston walked to where Mace was seated. "Or you can check out your partner."

Mace accepted the paperwork from Houston. After laying the file in his lap, he opened it, his hand trembling slightly. Clipped to the left side of the file folder was a full-color picture. His heart plummeted, then sped up. The photo showed a woman in a black body-fitting uniform with a mandarin collar around her slender throat. With her shoulders thrown back, she revealed her square, proud carriage. For a moment, his world centered on *her.* Oval face, golden skin, high cheekbones. As much as he didn't want to react, he couldn't help himself.

Mace had good instincts. They'd served him well as a recon marine, and they were operating overtime now. The woman in the picture wasn't smiling. There was no amusement in her cobalt colored eyes set with huge black pupils and a black ring around the iris. He was sure that she was a predator, a hunter. And her eyes shouted of her innate intelligence.

Ruthlessly, Mace scoured her photo for some telltale sign that she was weak or incapable of being the kind of partner he needed on this assignment.

From the file he knew she was military. What shocked him was the lock of hair dyed crimson amid blond tresses the color of a golden beach. The style shouted of her being highly independent.

Her mouth was calling to him. Gulping, he couldn't quite stop his heart from responding. Or his lower body, for that matter. Mace wondered what she would look like if she smiled. Chastising himself for the foolish thought, he began to think he'd been too long without a woman.

Tearing his gaze from the stunning photo, he began to read the biographical information on the right side of the file folder. Her name was Jessica Merrill. Her rank: CWO2—Chief Warrant Officer in the U.S. Army. Her current position: Apache helicopter gunship pilot. Mace quickly glanced at her photo once more. He'd been right: she was a class A hunter.

The logical side of his brain knew that her survivor abilities would be a good thing to have on the mission. His heart, however, rejected Jessica completely. He simply did *not* want a woman in his life right now, even on the job. He couldn't handle it.

Skimming the rest of the data from Jessica Merrill's U.S. Army personnel record, Mace discovered that she was a certified combat veteran, having flown for black ops in Peru for nearly four years and had two kills to her credit. She'd shot down two Russianmade Black Shark combat helicopters in the drug war being waged in that country. That was impressive. Again he looked at her face, those eagle eyes. Yes, he could tell she was real good at taking care of herself. Mace didn't want to admit it, but it seemed as if they'd chosen the right woman to go undercover with him. No-nonsense. Highly intelligent. Resourceful. All those attributes made a good agent.

Mace looked at her birth date: She was born February 5th. An Aquarian. Someone who was very humanitarian in a very practical way. Well, stopping drug dealers from flying cocaine out of Peru certainly fell under that requirement. He liked her loyalty to making the world a better place to live, her patriotism in subjecting herself daily to danger. And on top of everything else, he found her hauntingly beautiful in a wild, natural kind of way. An alpha female wolf without her mate...

"She looks adequate," Mace muttered, closing the file. Houston gave him a feral grin. Realizing he didn't know the details of the mission, Mace had the terrible feeling he'd just stepped into some sort of trap. An emotional one? God, he hoped not. His emotions were as taut as they had ever been. Every day was a struggle. Even now, two years after that horrific day when his life had fallen apart, he was just starting to get his footing back. He was finding a little light in the grayness of his life. But this? Her? Jessica Merrill? His hands pressed more surely against the folder in his lap, as if to hold it closed so it wouldn't spring open and bite him in his most vulnerable place: his heart.

"Adequate?" Houston said, a wry smile pulling at

one corner of his mouth. The major leaned back against Morgan's desk, his hands at his sides. "She's known as Wild Woman in the Black Jaguar Squadron. And for this mission you are going to need her, because she not only thinks outside the box, she invented the concept."

"I see."

"This mission to find Robert Marston and somehow get into his good graces is going to require finesse and creativity," Morgan added quietly. "Jessica Merrill is an accomplished officer, and her ability as a combat pilot is without equal. When the going gets tough, Chief Merrill gets the job done. That is why she was chosen for this mission. Her skills will strongly complement your knowledge of Hong Kong and your ability to speak Chinese."

He got it. He wasn't going on this mission without Jessica Merrill. "Well…" Mace cleared his throat and ran his fingertips across the file "…she looks Eurasian. I was wondering if someone in her family was from Asia?"

"She's part Cheyenne," Houston answered.

That explained the exotic tilt to her eyes and her broad, high cheekbones. Beautiful…

Mace didn't want to go there. Swallowing hard, he said, "When do I get to meet her? And when do we receive our final mission briefing?"

Morgan looked at his watch. "Chief Merrill is due here any minute."

"Since she's sure to have jet lag from her journey from Peru, the official briefing will be at 1400 hours tomorrow here in the war room," Houston added.

Mace heard the door behind him suddenly open and a woman say, "Chief Merrill is here. May I send her in?"

Morgan rose and buttoned his dark gray suit coat. "Yes, Jenny, please do. And ask if she's hungry or, better, wants a Krispy Creme doughnut," he said, grinning.

Mike Houston chuckled.

Heart pounding, Mace stood and turned around, the file clenched in his left hand. Jenny Wright, the assistant to these two top honchos of Perseus, stepped to one side of the door to ease it open wider.

When Jessica Merrill entered the room, Mace's throat went dry and his hand grew damp around the file. He felt all the heavy grayness wear away. And in its place, like the color of her short, straight hair, a blinding, brilliant sun bathed him. It was that red strip of hair that fell across the left side of her brow that shouted of her wildly independent nature. Mace blinked, unsure of what he saw. The color photo paled in comparison to the woman who stood before them, hands on her hips as she looked at them with a wicked grin.

"What is this? The boys club?" Jessica asked with a laugh.

"Well, it *was* the boys club," the man in the charcoal-gray suit said as he walked from behind the desk to shake her hand. "I'm Morgan Trayhern. Welcome to Perseus, Jessica. Allow me to introduce you to Mike Houston, number two in command here." He indicated a man wearing a dark blue blazer, white polo shirt and tan chinos. "And this," he said, gesturing to the man in a conservative suit and tie, "is CIA Agent Mason Phillips, your new partner. He likes to be called Mace."

Jessica nodded and strode forward to grip the hand that Mike Houston offered. "Howdy, Mike. Nice to meet you."

"Same here, Jessica. We're glad you've come."

Jessica turned to the CIA agent. Oh, the look on his face! Pure terror from what Jessie could see and sense around him. Thrusting out her hand, she said, "If looks could kill, Mace, I think I'd be dead on the floor." She squeezed his hand firmly and realized it was damp. Damp! The poor guy was sweating bullets! Feeling sorry for the dude because he obviously felt out of place, she smiled and saw his green eyes grow warm. But whether the reaction was due to her gesture or their contact, she wasn't sure. "But don't worry, I'm no fainting violet."

The scent of her perfume, spicy, just like her, embraced Mace. Tongue-tied, he lost himself in her dancing blue eyes, which had flecks of sunlight in their depths. "I…it's very nice to meet you, Chief Merrill."

Mace knew he sounded like an embarrassed teenager on his first date. He saw amusement sparkle in her eyes and lift lips that bore only lip balm. She wore no makeup, but she had need for none.

She wore modest pearl earrings in her small earlobes and a dainty gold necklace adorned her slim throat. She wore low-rider jeans and a bright red tank top that exposed her midriff. The tank revealed her collarbones and hinted at the small breasts beneath. With a start Mace realized that she wasn't wearing a bra. And she didn't seem to care that he could see her nipples against the silken material. Gulping, he finally released her hand.

"Chief Merrill?" Jessie hooted. "Let's cut the official stuff, okay? Just call me Wild Woman or Jessie. I answer to either."

Mace felt outgunned, outmanned and outmaneuvered, and he'd only just met the woman. Jessica Merrill was like a blinding sunbeam, and the whole room radiated with her warmth, benevolence and towering self-confidence. And for the first time in two years he felt his heart opening.

Chapter 2

"Thanks, Mr. Trayhern," Jessie said as she accepted the chair that he offered next to Agent Phillips.

"Call me Morgan, please. Are you hungry? Thirsty? Jenny can get you anything you'd like from our cafeteria."

Shaking her head, she grinned and said, "Sir, no thanks. Jenny kindly offered, as well, but as I told her, I stuffed myself like a little porker on the flight from Peru. I love good food and the airline made plenty available. I'll probably get hungry again in a couple of hours." She patted her tummy and laughed.

Something niggled at Jessie and she turned to look at the CIA agent. She could detect censure in his hooded green eyes. Toward *her?* Hell, he didn't even know her.

"Can't we even interest you in some good Peruvian coffee?" Houston teased, forcing Jessie's thoughts back to the meeting in progress. He handed her the mission folder.

"Oh, now *that* I would love! Thanks." Her response earned a smile from the man known as the Jaguar God in Peru. "To tell you the truth, Mike, I feel like I'm sitting in front of two great legends. Morgan, you're as famous as the presidents carved on Mount Rushmore."

"I hope I don't look that old?"

Jessie laughed at his good-natured teasing. "Hardly!" Morgan Trayhern was a helluva man, and he had a helluva good sense of humor. But then, in Jessie's experience, most military people relied on humor to get them through the sometimes daily reality of facing death.

"Well," Mike murmured, coming to stand next to Morgan's chair, "we are old by military standards but we like to think we have savvy gained from those experiences."

"You do, indeed," Jessie said. Again, she felt something. What was it? Turning, she looked over at the agent. His eyes were downcast. His large, square hands were flattened over a red folder on his lap. What was his problem? Turning away, Jessie heard the door open.

Jenny Wright smiled warmly as she entered the room with a tray filled with steaming cups of coffee, a pitcher of cream and a bowl of sugar. She set the tray on a small coffee table near a leather couch.

"This is so cool," Jessie said. "I can smell it's Peruvian clear over here!"

Houston joined Jenny at the coffee service, where they began to take orders. Chuckling, he said, "There's more where this came from. I have my own special connections for the good stuff." He walked over to Jessie and handed her a cup. "There's nothing in the world like South American coffee."

"I second that," she said, accepting the strong black coffee. Inhaling the fragrant steam, she closed her eyes and murmured, "Ahhh, heaven on earth…"

Cradling the fragile white china cup in her slender hands, Jessie reminded Mace of a long, graceful bird in flight. No more than five foot six inches tall, she was lean and obviously in top condition, with small breasts and a long torso. Womanly hips were just beneath the sinful jeans poured around those long legs of hers.

"Mr. Phillips?" Jenny Wright smiled down at him. "Would you like to savor the best coffee in the world?"

"Yes...thank you." He took the proffered cup.

"Cream? Sugar?"

"No, thanks..."

"That's one mark for you."

Hearing Jessie's husky words, Mace turned toward her. Her eyes were dancing with humor.

"Excuse me?"

Good grief! This dude was insufferably polite. For a moment, she allowed her intuition to give her a reading on him. The first emotion that registered was incredible sadness surrounding him like a heavy cloak. It was such a startling revelation that Jessie instantly closed down her all-terrain sensory radar. Yes, sadness was what she saw in Mace Phillips's large, guarded eyes. A sorrow so fathomless that Jessie felt for a moment as if she was drowning in it.

"Taking your coffee black. That's good. I like a man who can handle it hot and intense." She lifted her cup in a silent toast, knowing that she'd resorted to teasing to lighten the mood.

A warning sounded deep inside Mace. For so long, his heart had felt chained. Yet when Wild Woman grinned, revealing even white teeth and those willful lips lifting ever so slightly, he felt...hope? *No. Impossible.* There was *no* hope for him. Whatever he'd had was snuffed out years ago. Still, his heart sighed as that small ray of light, for just a second, pierced his inner darkness and unexpectedly touched him. Warmly.

"Well, now that formalities are out of the way," Morgan said, commanding the group's attention, "I'd ask that you go over the mission file tonight at your condos. We're putting you in the Blue section of the complex, and across the hall from one another. Jenny will take you to your quarters in a few minutes."

Holding her cup in one hand, Jessie flipped open the file.

"Jessie," Houston said, resting against the front of Morgan's desk to face her, "you were specifically chosen for this mission because of a vision that Kai Alseoun had. You know about that, don't you?"

"Yes, sir, I do. I met Kai in Peru. I'm aware of what's going down."

"Good." Mike motioned to Agent Phillips. "If you feel up to it tonight, could you fill Mace in? If not, don't worry about it."

Shrugging, Jessie said, "I'm too wired to sleep right now, so I can spend an hour connecting the dots. No problem."

"A can-do woman," Morgan murmured, pleased. "That's the spirit we like around here. Teamwork."

"Oh, I'm a great team player," Jessie said with a laugh. She stole another look at her glum, retiring partner and wondered if he ever smiled. "I saw a nice little Chinese restaurant in Phillipsburg on my way here in the cab. How about I buy you some dim sum and we can chat?"

"I'll buy," Mace said.

He threw out the remark as if laying down a gauntlet.

"I said it first. Whoever says it first gets to buy." Jessie leaned toward him, narrowing her eyes, daring him to fight her. Maybe that was what he needed: someone to light a fire under him. No problem. She was damn good at doing that.

"Whoa, you two." Houston held up his hands. "No fighting. Remember, the enemy is out there, not in here."

Mace held Jessie's stare. Her eyes were filled with wicked amusement and pleaded with him to take her on. Well, this wasn't the place. Houston was right about that. Mace took a sip of the hot coffee. Burning his tongue, he nearly choked, but wasn't going to let any of them know. "Fine," he said gruffly, "you can buy me dinner this one time."

Jessie smiled wolfishly. "How very kind of you, Agent Phillips."

"So tell me about this vision that Kai Alseoun had," Mace suggested after they had been comfortably seated in a small red leather booth at the Golden Dragon. The noise level in the crowded Chinese restaurant was surprisingly low. Waiters and waitresses dressed in crisply ironed black pants and white shirts fluttered among the twenty booths and thirty tables in service like unobtrusive butterflies as Mace and Jessie ate heartily from a large lazy Susan holding at least eight different dishes. Jessie had a voracious appetite. And she could handle a pair of chopsticks with the best of them, Mace noticed, impressed. As a combat pilot, she probably ran on adrenaline all day long. Such stress could eat up energy at a horrific rate, Mace knew.

Jessie popped a piece of Mongolian beef into her mouth and savored it for a long moment. Clearly she wasn't one of those women who were always eating salads to maintain their weight.

"Kai is pureblood Eastern Cherokee," she said. "One of the first Native American women to fly in combat. When she was in the navy, she flew the F-14 Tomcat. She saw action in Afghanistan and Iraq and has two kills to her credit."

Raising his brows, Mace said, "That's really something."

"No shit, Sherlock."

Jessie picked daintily at some popcorn shrimp with her slender fingers and Mace found himself mesmerized. There was such excruciating femininity to this woman…who had two kills to her own credit. Despite her brash remark, Mace didn't see opposite him a tough combat pilot. What he saw was a deliciously vivacious woman whose smile was bringing warmth to the frozen wasteland within him. Looks were deceiving, he knew. Jessica Merrill reminded him of an impish sprite, an ethereal being. But she had a solid build and was all woman. Mace hoped she hadn't seen him lusting over just that fact.

"Now, you aren't gonna be one of those dudes who says to me, 'Wild Woman, you got a potty mouth. Stow it.' Are you?" She laughed huskily.

"Do I look shocked?"

"Yes. I know you CIA types are supposed to be all starch and aplomb, but could you relax a little? You're wound up too tight."

A smile pulled at one corner of his mouth as he regarded Jessie, who continued to nibble at the shrimp. When she licked her fingers, his lower body cramped. He felt the first stirrings of desire and realized that he hadn't really been alive for a long time. This woman, with her uninhibited nature, was touching him as he thought no woman ever could again.

"I've been cooped up in a room for three months doing translation work, so my people skills are a little rusty."

Chuckling, she said, "Oh, no problem, dude. Hang around me for forty-eight and I'll get you loosey-goosey."

"Loosey-goosey?"

"Yeah, an aviator term. You know, being all relaxed. Having no cares in the world."

"You can manage that in forty-eight hours?" he asked dryly, picking at the Mongolian beef with his chopsticks.

Jessica slapped at his chopsticks with her own, the beef falling with a splat back into the dish. Leaning forward she whispered, "Wanna bet?"

The smile on her face was wolfish. Her eyes were narrowed. Challenging. Just asking for trouble. Pulling his chopsticks slowly from beneath hers, he said, "I don't make bets."

"What a stick-in-the-mud you are!"

"Are you always this kind to the people you work with?"

"Oh, no. I'm *worse!*" She began prodding the back of his hand with her chopsticks, beef juice dripping over the hairy expanse.

Jessie absolutely delighted in disrupting Mace's stuffy, conservative world. She watched him jerk his hand away, his straight brows drawing into a line of displeasure, as he grabbed the linen napkin from his lap to wipe off the liquid.

"I'll bet you were one of those brats as a kid who used to have food fights."

"Now, how did you guess that, government man?" Jessie whispered.

She continued to lean forward, both elbows on the red-linen-draped table, her mouth pulled into a grin, her eyes alive with mirth. More than anything, Mace liked that red streak of fire in her blond hair. *Wild Woman. Yeah, no kidding, dude. She's for real. Are you?*

He didn't want to answer that question.

"And what did *you* do as a little boy, I wonder? Were you the type that hid in the background and watched others?"

"You're dangerous with those chopsticks," he said, replacing the napkin on his lap.

"Anything can be a weapon. You ought to know that."

"Oh, I do. You are."

"Yeah?"

"Yeah." He eyed the dim sum. "Are you going to deny me food?"

"Maybe…"

He liked the sultry look she gave him, her lips pouty, before she leaned back in the booth.

"Are you for real?" he asked her.

"What you see is what you get."

"And you're like this all the time?"

"Yeah. You oughta ask Snake, my copilot. We shake and bake out there in the skies over Peru together. We do a sky dance that keeps us in stitches up there while we're huntin' for the bad guys."

"Snake? Is that a woman or a man?"

"A woman, of course. We have a mostly female combat squadron in Peru. We are constantly being stalked by Russian mercenaries paid by the drug lords to fly Black Shark combat helos after us."

Pride was unmistakable in her voice and in the way she squared her shoulders and lifted her chin.

"You're a warrior of the first order, then."

"We all are down there. It's a dangerous business, lemme tell you. The Apache can't get the signature on this beast, so we're always flying with one eye on the drug planes and one eye rubbernecking around the sky so we don't get made into a crispy critter by one of 'em."

"Amazing," Mace murmured, reaching for the bowl of Mongolian beef. This time, she didn't attack his chopsticks.

Sipping her green tea, Wild Woman grinned at him. "I am amazing. My sisters in arms are equally amazing. We're a damn amazing group, come to think of it. The world may not know about us, but we sure as hell know what we're doing for the world."

"You're pretty cocky."

"Oh, I've been called a lot worse," Jessie said, chortling. As she sipped more of the tea, she watched Mace carefully pick at the chicken with his chopsticks. "I wonder, have you ever done a spontaneous thing in your life, Phillips?"

Nettled, he said, "You can call me Mace. And the answer is yes."

"So you have been spontaneous?"

"Once."

"Well, that's encouraging."

"Don't let it go to your head."

Giggling, Jessie seized another popcorn shrimp with her chopsticks, dipped it in the hot wasabi sauce and drew the delicious morsel into her mouth. Sighing with contentment, she said, "Somehow, I don't think it will."

Becoming serious, Mace said, "You never told me about Kai's vision. What does it have to do with you?"

"With *us*," Jessie corrected.

She laid aside her chopsticks and folded her hands before her on the table. Was there ever a moment that Mace didn't look serious? Gathering her thoughts, she said, "When Kai returned home from the navy, she went on a vision quest."

"A vision quest?"

Jessie threw up her hands. "Oh, I keep forgetting Anglos don't know these terms. When a person needs guidance regarding what direction to take in life, we have a ceremony called a vision quest. After purifying in a sweat lodge, the person goes someplace remote, like a mountain, for four days with just a blanket and a sacred pipe. You have no water. No food. All you do, hour after hour, is pray for a vision. If the Great Spirit knows you're sincere, you will be granted one. And that's basically what happened to Kai. She needed a new life direction. Only—" Jessie grinned "—the vision she got was one she wasn't expecting.

"The Great Spirit showed her the location of three crystal totems stolen from the Eastern Cherokee Nation. All are thousands of years old and hold incredible power. Now, Kai didn't know that they had been stolen from the medicine man's house. So after sharing this vision with her grandmother, a Cherokee elder, all hell broke loose. Kai's vision charged her with finding the first totem, the Paint Clan mask. With financing from Medusa, the company under the Perseus umbrella headed by Mike Houston, Kai and another Eastern Cherokee, Jake Stands Alone Carter, traveled to Australia to find it."

"Did they?"

Nodding, Jessie said, "Yes, they got it back for the nation. Now, Kai's vision revealed that two other women were supposed to track down the other two totems. My friend Snake just found the second one, the crystal star, in Peru." Jessie ran her fingers through the crimson streak in her hair. "Kai didn't know what to make of me, but when she saw me with Snake, saw my hair, she knew I was the third woman in her vision, the one meant to go after the Wolf Clan totem."

Mace shook his head. "That's an astounding story."

"I bet you government types would pooh-pooh it and send us to the funny farm if we shared it with you."

"We deal with the more black and white scenarios."

"There is *nothing* rational in our world," Jessie said. "You just *think* there is. My mother is a Cheyenne medicine woman. I was trained in our traditions and I know for a fact that there is more magic and more mystery occurring than you rational types will ever know. I've seen it with my own two eyes, and I've experienced it, as well."

"I understand that's why Major Houston formed Medusa. He said Perseus needed a branch that dealt with more than just the 'rational.'"

"Right. Major Houston is not only South American Indian, he is also a trained shaman. He knows metaphysics is part and parcel of our lives, and I, for one, am glad to see he was able to create Medusa."

"I'm just saying that I have a feeling the people I work for would die laughing over this vision quest explanation."

"And yet Kai's vision accurately showed where two of the three crystals were."

"So, where's the third one?"

"On an island off China's mainland."

"That has to be Hong Kong. Or Macao."

"Kai believes it's Hong Kong. Plus, Robert Marston, who we now know is the mastermind behind these thefts, has a multimillion-dollar villa in Hong Kong. He's a known collector of Native American artifacts and he's not above stealing or killing to get what he wants."

"This is sounding so off the wall...." Mace began. He saw her flat look of frustration. "I don't do airy fairy stuff."

"You don't have to. I'll be the one handling that end of the stick."

"I will be very interested to see what this briefing brings tomorrow afternoon."

Rubbing her hands together, Jessie whispered gleefully, "That makes two of us, dude! I'll bet by the end of it, your jaw is gonna drop!"

Chapter 3

"This mission is way beyond anything you would normally expect," Mike Houston told Mace and Jessie. It was 1400 and he was pleased that they'd shown up on time to the second to settle in for the briefing.

Jenny Wright began distributing packets of information.

"Jenny is handing you the rest of the intel. What we gave you yesterday was the broad overview of the mission. Thanks, Jenny."

She smiled. "Of course. Anything else, Mike?"

He returned her smile. "I think we've got it covered, Jenny. Thanks."

Nodding, she turned and strode to the door, shutting it quietly behind her as she left the room.

"Open up the packets," Mike said once they were alone.

Jessie kept her eyes downcast as she spread the contents in front of her on the table. When she did look up, she caught Mace staring at her. She wasn't sure if it was censure, shock or something else she saw in his expression. After their dinner last night, she'd been experiencing a range of reactions, too, but she recognized immediately that it must be fatigue from flying.

Of course, today she wore a pair of loose fitting red cotton trousers, a red tank top with a white, long-sleeved blouse over it and a pair of snazzy yellow suspenders. Red and yellow were her favorite colors, so why not wear them together?

That was it. She was just too wild, free and spontaneous for the likes of this ultraconservative, button-down dude.

"What you've got in front of you," Mike said, "is a dossier on Robert Marston. He's Canadian, born in Toronto. He's eighty years old and a billionaire. Marston owns more media outlets in cable television, magazines, videotape and film than anyone else in the world. His home is Toronto, but for the last ten years he's been working out of his Hong Kong villa, known as Lihua."

"In Cantonese," Mace said, directing his explanation to Jessie, "that means 'beautiful flower.'"

She smiled at him. "Cool, dude. Thank you."

Mace felt a warm flush creeping up his neck. All Jessie had to do was turn on that ten thousand megawatt smile of hers and he melted like a puddle of water around her feet. Clearing his throat, he muttered, "You're welcome."

"Well, if everything goes as planned, you'll be at Lihua shortly. From here on out, though, you need to study like hell and commit everything about Marston to memory," Houston said, pointing at the dossiers in front of them. "We've coordinated our intel with the help of Interpol, the FBI and CIA. I worked with the head of the CIA's Southeast Asia operations to compile what we have on Marston."

Jessie looked at the color photo of the man. Robert Marston had watery blue eyes. Beneath his pasty bald pate white hair rimmed his head. Gold wire-rimmed glasses perched on his beaklike nose. "I dunno about you two, but this guy looks like death warmed over."

"Like a ghoul," Mace quietly agreed.

"He appears to be wheelchair bound," Jessie remarked.

"Marston has Parkinson's disease," Houston explained. "He's had it since age fifty. It's his fly in the ointment. He has used his money to try and buy his health back. Ironically, all the money in the world can't give him what he needs most."

"Doesn't look like he succeeded," Jessie said. "This dude looks more dead than alive, if this is a recent photo." Intuitively, she shivered. "Ugh!"

"What?" Mace saw her wrap her arms around herself as she made a face at Marston's photo before her.

"This dude gives me the creeps. Big-time." She looked up at Mike. "What is it about him? I feel like he's a spider that slowly trolls out his silken line, sneaks it around you and then tightens it before you know you've been caught."

"Very good, Jessie. You've pretty much described his corporate tactics to a T."

She picked up the photograph to examine it more closely. "There's more to this dude, Mike. I can *feel* it. My radar is waving red flags all over the place."

Houston nodded and said, "I'm happy to know your gut instinct is operating. You're right, he's a master manipulator. Although he looks old and frail in this photo, don't ever think that he isn't intelligent and wily as a weasel."

"That's probably how he made his billions," Mace said. He couldn't help studying Wild Woman. She was fascinating to watch, with her face constantly changing, mirroring whatever she felt or thought. And she was beautiful. Wild and free as a mustang. What he'd give to have those feelings.

Houston opened another file and handed them more color photos. "This is Lihua. Your mission will be to get inside its doors and make contact with Robert Marston. To assist you, we have secured the services of an important contact in Hong Kong. His name is Ji Yaozong. He's a millionaire corporate software owner.

"Three years ago, Ji's oldest son, who was ten at the time, was kidnapped and held for ransom in China. Ji contacted Perseus and we sent a team to rescue the boy. We succeeded and Ji told us that if we ever needed a favor, he'd be there for us."

"I see," Mace murmured. He shifted his focus to Jessie. "The firstborn son in a Chinese family is a big deal. He will be groomed to take over the father's business, and be expected to pass on the family dynasty to the next generation."

"Right," Mike said. "The kidnappers didn't take Ji's second son or firstborn daughter. They knew what they were doing. They were asking for ten million U.S. dollars for the son's safe return. Ji called us because sometimes, when someone is kidnapped in Asia, the money is sent and the victim is murdered. Ji knew that."

"That's nasty business," Jessie murmured. "Mike, what is Ji doing for us?"

"He's gotten you an invitation to Robert Marston's Wild West gala." Mike handed Jessie a crisp linen envelope tastefully embossed in gold. "Mr. and Mrs. Creighton Webb are invited to the Wild West barbecue that he's hosting three days from now."

Opening the invitation carefully, Jessie registered the fake names printed on the envelope. "This is very nice paper," she murmured, running her fingertips across the insert's creamy smooth surface.

"That's eighteen carat gold Marston used for the printing," Houston said.

"So, we're a married couple?" Mace asked, refusing to let that detail go unquestioned.

"Yes, and multimillionaire software owners. As we speak, Ji is having one of his helicopters repainted with the name and logo of your company, Titan Industries. We want you to make a splash with Marston. Get his attention. Jessie will fly you two to Marston's helipad at Lihua. That should make a statement."

"Wouldn't Marston know about Titan Industries if we were that big and rich?" Wild Woman demanded.

"Ordinarily, yes. And the CIA is working right now to ensure that Titan Industries is legit when Marston decides to check you out. And he will," Mike warned them. "You're going to tell him that all your recent software designs are sold to the U.S. government and are top secret in nature. When they are, not much gets out in the business world about such corporations. The CIA is putting information into Pentagon computers and the procurement officer computer, which has all contractor bids and awards, so that when Marston wants to get info, it's there."

"And just how strong is our background?" Mace demanded. He knew all too well what a flimsy cover story would mean for them. He didn't want to be left hung out to dry.

Houston grinned. "Trust me when I tell you that no Perseus mission moves forward without guaranteed covers so that agents can't be spotted as fakes. Titan Industries is already in the Pentagon computers. And we know that's where Marston will look."

"It sounds like Mace here will get all the fun. What's the wife doing in this game, Mike?"

"Don't worry, you're not relegated to the background. In fact, you're the person the whole mission depends on."

"Oh?"

"As you no doubt briefed Mace, your ultimate objective is to locate the wolf clan totem. We know from Ji, who has been to Marston's yearly parties, that Marston has a huge three-room building devoted entirely to his artifacts. The outer room is the one where he escorts all his cronies to show off his vast collection of indigenous artifacts. The second room he reserves for 'special' people. Ji has never been invited into that room."

"You said three. What's in the third room?" Mace asked.

Shrugging, Mike said, "Ji and I figure that the more important artifacts, mostly stolen, are kept in room three. But we don't know. No one knows." He turned to Wild Woman. "That's where you come in. Your job is to infiltrate the second and third rooms. Jessie, you need to get into Marston's good graces and convince him to take you through all three rooms."

"I *like* it!" she crowed, lifting her fist in a victory sign. "Besides, I love getting into a costume!"

"Well, you will be," Mike said, smiling. He directed their attention to another sheet in the packet. "That's your cover. Some of it is true, which is good. For instance, we know your mother is a medicine woman on the Cheyenne Reservation, Jessie."

"That's right."

"Well, we're going to use this information as a hook to get to Marston. When you fly in for his barbecue, you're going to be dressed unlike any other guest. Jenny has what you'll need packed for you at her desk, and you'll take it with you."

"Great!" Excited, she grinned at Mace. All she got in response was a frown. What a party pooper! She looked back at Houston. "Tell all, Mike. I'm all ears," she said, chuckling. "Wolf ears."

"Ji said over a hundred of the rich and famous will be at the party, so we needed something to ensure you make one helluva entrance to snag Marston's interest. You'll look Native American in every respect. Black wig. Braids."

"I'll dress like an Indian going to ceremony."

"Correct."

Frowning, Mace said, "Wait…what's that mean? I'm not Indian and you two are. Care to elaborate?"

Chuckling, Jessie reached out and patted his hand. She liked touching this CIA agent. Instantly, she saw his green eyes flare with surprise and then something else. Pleasure, maybe? Her smile grew as she curled her fingers around his large, strong ones. "Tut, tut, Mace. We aren't going to keep you out of the loop." She wanted to continue to hold his hand but decided the gesture was enough of a shock to him. Releasing it, she said, "When we go to ceremony, we wear special duds. In my case, I have a beautiful hand-beaded deerskin vest that I wear over a shirt. Shirts are usually made from calico material and can be any color. I love red, so I have a red one. Thirty red ribbons hang from the yoke, front and back. I have a pair of knee-high buffalo-skin boots with elk-bone buttons. And I have a special buffalo horn choker."

"You were asked to bring all your ceremonial gear with you," Mike said.

"And I did. But I sure like the idea of wearing a black wig with long braids. That's awesome!" she said, patting her short blond hair.

Smiling, Mike turned to Mace, who was looking confused. "By having Jessie dress in her people's ceremonial gear, I feel that Robert Marston will zero in on her like a bee to honey. As his dossier showed, he's absolutely enthralled with Native Americans and is no stranger to them and their ways."

"Which is another reason to have me in on this gig," Wild Woman said, rubbing her hands and smiling. "I *am* Cheyenne Indian. Well, fifty percent."

"You *look* Indian enough to pass muster with Marston," Mike said. "He'll know you aren't a fullblood, but that doesn't matter. You'll walk the talk. And—" he extracted more photos from the packet to show them "—this should get him enthused over you, Jessie."

She looked at the pictures. "That's a medicine pouch," she said, pointing to one of the two images. "And that one is a Grandmother's necklace."

Mike smiled. "Right."

Before Mace could voice the questions she knew he had, Jessie said, "Every Indian has a medicine bag, which reflects them on a deeply personal and spiritual level. What is in it is privy only to them. Some contain shells, stones, feathers or other things from nature. Medicine bags are very powerful. Some are superpowerful, depending upon who they belong to."

"The bags of medicine people top this hierarchy of importance," Houston added. "And some people resort to stealing to get them."

"Power begets power," Wild Woman said.

"And the Grandmother's necklace?" Mace asked, pointing to the photo of a long string of beads that looked to be turquoise, agate and amber.

"This is a necklace that is passed down from one generation to another in a medicine family," Mike answered. "The power in it is terrific. The firstborn daughter of each generation is given this when she becomes a woman. Such a necklace is worn at every ceremony, so it holds the power of hundreds, if not thousands, of ceremonies. And I'm betting the farm that Marston will salivate over these ceremonial items you'll be wearing." Houston grinned sourly. "If we know Marston, he's going to want what you got."

"He won't get it, though," Jessie declared.

"Right. But you'll use these items to convince him to let you see all three rooms of his museum. You need to play dumb, though. Marston is so damn arrogant that he needs to believe he's smarter than everyone else."

"Aren't they always that way?" she said. She

smiled warmly across the table at Mace. "Do you understand a little more now? Not feeling so left out?"

Shrugging, he admitted, "Your culture is alien to me, but interesting."

"I'll fill you in more on the flight to Hong Kong," Jessica promised.

She liked the fact that Mace seemed genuinely interested. His eyes were a bit brighter and that made her feel good. Anything that lifted the dark shadows from their depths made her heart glow. She didn't know why.

Early this morning when she'd awakened, she'd lain in bed, simply enjoying the peace and quiet, and thought about *him*. Mace was a reliable, responsible person. She could see that. But it bothered her that he never smiled. Was it because he'd been stuck away in that same office job for three months? She'd go bats handling that kind of an assignment, too. But her heart told her that there was something else...something so awful that he carried it around with him. That *something* was what she wanted to understand about Mace.

Whether he knew it or not, he was on *her* radar screen and she was going to use the twenty-hour flight to Hong Kong to find out why he was so sad. Their mission objective notwithstanding, her secret goal was to make him smile. Yep, she had Mace Phillips in her gun sights and he was hers.

Chapter 4

"I love living in the lap of luxury," Jessie confided to Mace as they sat next to each other in the "hump" of the 747 jumbo jet en route to China. The stairs from the first class section led up to this portion of the airliner, where they could converse in privacy. "The seat is *so* roomy! And I love the fact it can be made into a bed so we can stretch out and sleep."

Running her fingers up and down the buttery black leather of the armrest, she grinned over at him. Jenny Wright had not only chosen his impeccably tailored suit and her pale pink silk suit as "travel clothes," but their luggage was packed with designer duds. Since they were undercover as multimillionaires, that meant every detail of the mission had to be perfect. Anyone snooping into their bags would find expensive clothes from Italy, France and Germany. Jessie was just happy to be wearing civilian clothes instead of her one-piece Black Jaguar Squadron flight suit. Of course, the black wig she wore and newly dyed eyebrows to match would take some getting used to.

Mace managed a slight smile. "I like the fact we're in the hump alone."

Jessie pulled the half-empty bottle of champagne from the ice bucket and poured herself another glassful. "You want more?"

"Me? No."

"Oh, come on! You're not on duty now! I mean, we're alone up here, Mace. You need to let your hair down, my friend." Jessie grabbed his glass and filled it with the golden champagne. "Here, drink up!"

"Do you always nag everyone?" he asked dryly, taking the glass by the stem.

Giggling like a schoolgirl, she replaced the bottle in the bucket between their massive seats and picked up her glass. "I try to. Does it show?"

Sipping the dry champagne, Mace watched as Jessie drank half her glass. "Just a little."

There wasn't anything halfway about Wild

Woman. She embraced life. He ran away from it. She took pleasure in the smallest of things, like licking the rim of her glass to get the last taste of the expensive champagne on her tongue. He never took pleasure in anything. Waking up every day was an effort, not something to be looked forward to with gusto and vibrancy.

"Ohh, Mace, you're just being too darn nice!" Jessie wriggled around in her chair to sit sideways, drawing up her knees and propping her chin on them as she watched him. She liked his square face, those dark black brows. Most of all, she liked to look into his large green eyes. They were wide apart, which was an indication of intelligence in horses and, she believed, in people. When he wasn't brooding, Mace's eyes were an evergreen color, reminiscent of her beloved Rocky Mountains swathed in forests. Jessie found herself wanting to dive into his eyes, to immerse herself in that incredible color and become one with him.

Abruptly, she sobered. *Become one with him?* What was she thinking? She had a healthy sex drive, no doubt about it. But she didn't chase after men just for sexual satisfaction. She was as picky about a man in her life as Snake, her combat partner. And, like Snake, Jessie looked for long-term emotional commitment, not bed hopping. Something told her that Mace was a man who not only honored a relationship, but nurtured it so that it would go on forever. Glancing at his left hand, she observed the fake wedding ring that he wore for their undercover assignment. Surely he had a *real* significant other. Jessie couldn't even imagine that someone as handsome and responsible as Mace would be single, much less available.

"I know we have a cover story," Jessie said, waving her hand airily, "but I'd like to know about *you,* Mace. Where were you born?"

Mace sat back in his seat, feeling the champagne work through him, loosening him up a little more than he was comfortable being. He rested his glass on the arm of the seat and gazed over at her rapt features. "Portland, Oregon. You?"

"Lame Deer, Montana. On the Northern Cheyenne Res. You got brothers? Sisters?"

"I have two younger sisters, Marge and Susan. You?"

"Oh, you were the older brother! No wonder you're so serious all the time!" She chuckled, then drained her glass. Picking up the bottle again, she divided the remaining champagne between Mace's glass and her own before raising hers to him. "Here's to older brothers who catch hell for all their siblings' activities."

Mace wanted to withdraw, which was his usual ploy, but gazing into her sparkling blue eyes filled with passion and life, he decided to hell with that. He was feeling good. How long had it been since he'd felt this relaxed? And in the middle of an undercover op? He laughed to himself and watched as Jessie wriggled around in her seat, trying to get comfy, one slender leg hanging over the arm, her nylon clad toe brushing his chair. Obviously a child of the earth, she'd kicked off her white leather sandals at the first possible moment.

"I know about the oldest kid syndrome," she informed him in a wicked whisper. "You see, I was the oldest, too!"

"You had younger siblings?" She'd probably played hell on them growing up, Mace thought.

"I was the *only* one!" she said, clamping a hand over her mouth to muffle her laughter.

Caught off guard by her trap, he smiled. "You're good, you know that?"

Preening, Wild Woman said, "I know. Thank you."

"And your parents didn't raise a spoiled little princess, did they?"

"Very good, Mace! I knew you had it in you!"

"Tell me about living on a reservation. What was that like?"

Tipping her glass up, she stuck out her tongue to catch the last droplets of champagne. Licking her lips with satisfaction, she said, "Well, I'm the result of living there. I'm a wild mustang, free by nature, kicking butt, taking no prisoners." Leaning toward him, she whispered, "And what was it like to be raised *off* a reservation, white boy?"

A chuckle rumbled through his chest. The flight attendant had left another bottle of champagne chilling—just in case they wanted more. Mace was sure that she hadn't wanted to run up and down the stairs to take care of them, and that was fine with him. Easing the full bottle out of the bucket, he said, "More?"

"What do you think, guy?" Smiling widely, she held out her glass.

"Unequivocally yes." He worked the cork from the bottle and filled it. "I guess I had that coming. That remark about being raised on a reservation versus anywhere in America. Point taken."

"Thank you," Wild Woman said. She lifted her glass in another toast as he refilled his own. "To you, Mace. Cheers."

Replacing the bottle in the bucket between them, Mace downed about half the glass in one good, healthy swallow. The bubbles tickled going down his throat. "This *is* good," he said.

"I take it you don't drink much?"

"You took it right."

"Nine to fiver, I'll bet. And then you spend an hour in D.C. traffic on the way home to your apartment, pull out a TV dinner, sit down with the paper or watch the news as you eat."

Amazed at her insight, Mace stared at her. "How…"

Raising her eyebrows, Wild Woman said, "You men are so easy to read." She emptied her glass, then leaned over to refill it.

"You don't do that?"

"Until a few days ago, I was twenty-four on and twenty-four off. Try that for three and a half years, white bread. No city drive. No newspaper. No television."

Mace laughed. "White bread? Is that what you call us white folks? Is that an Indian expression?"

"Among others," she answered. "I was being nice."

"I guess I should take that as a compliment. How about you? Have you ever been called anything other than Wild Woman?"

"It's always been Wild Woman, although, my Cheyenne name is Hotamemâsêhao'o, which means Crazy Dog."

"Helluva name. Sounds rabid."

"Oh, as a little one, I was a hellion at times. But the medicine woman that named me at birth told my mother I was a 'way shower,' someone who broke new ground so that other women could follow."

"A role model, then." Mace couldn't take his eyes

off of her. Jessie's cheeks were flushed, her eyes bright. Her luscious lips beckoned to him.

"Bingo."

"So, not so rabid, after all."

"I'm not some tame little poodle, Mr. Phillips— er, Mace."

"Poodle? No, I'd never see you as a poodle."

"What then?" Jessie was interested in how he saw her. She liked the mind game she was playing with him now. He played it very well.

Shrugging, Mace finished his champagne. "How about a Doberman pinscher?"

"Okay...I can live with that. Why that breed?"

"My parents had a Dobe for a long time. Cookie. She was absolutely loyal to us, but God help anyone who came to the door who wasn't part of her 'family.' At the slightest threat to us she was all teeth and jaws."

"So, you see me as loyal? Defending my family?"

"Absolutely."

Jessie yawned. "You know what? I'm going to take a quick nap. Can we pick up where we left off after I snooze awhile, Mace?"

"No problem. In fact, I'm going to get some shut-eye myself. If anything interesting happens, wake me?"

Closing her eyes, she murmured, "You'll be the first to know, pardner...."

* * *

Jessie was in a very dark place. Everything was quiet. Deadly quiet. Squinting to try to get her bearings, she felt an internal tug, an instinctive urge to move forward. The light, if it could be called that, was like a dusk just before the cape of the night fell over the land. Nothing was easy to see. Her heart began a slow pounding.

Bothered by the sense of danger in the tomblike place, Jessie urged herself to press on. She thought she saw something behind a thick glass display window. Yes…it was. My God, it was the wolf clan totem! As she drew near, placing her hands on the cool, flat surface of the window, her breath caught. Light was emanating from within the crystal as it slowly rotated on a dark green velvet cushion.

The object was mesmerizing. As she stood transfixed by the totem's throbbing glow, she began to see numbers slowly congealing in her mind. They played over and over again. Big red numbers: 2241.

It must be important, she thought. But why numbers? Was the crystal "talking" to her? She wasn't sure.

The low sound of the jet engine penetrated her dream, easing her back to wakefulness. Lifting a hand, she rubbed her eyes and yawned. How long had she slept?

"You got four hours' sleep," Mace said.

"I did? Wow. It felt like I just dropped off a few

minutes ago." How handsome he looked. "How much shut-eye did you get?"

Shrugging, he said, "Probably three and a half hours. You were sleeping like there was no tomorrow." He didn't want to admit to Jessie that it had been pure pleasure watching her sleep. She was an angel in repose. Beautiful. And he yearned for her in ways that surprised him.

Standing to stretch, she said, "I had the oddest dream, Mace." She told him about seeing the wolf clan totem. "Those numbers mean something, but I don't know what," she said, frowning.

Mace wrote the numbers on a pad of paper. "It may be nothing, but I know now dreams have meaning. We'll keep these close—just in case."

"Good idea." She smiled sleepily at him. "Let's see, I wanted to talk about *you* before I zonked out. We were talking about dogs, right? You know what breed you remind me of?"

He saw the devilishness in her eyes. "I'm afraid to ask."

"Oh, come on, Mace! Be a risk taker. Ask me!"

He took his time before answering. "Okay, you bring out the best in me, Jessie. What dog do I remind you of?"

"A bloodhound."

Mace didn't know whether to laugh or to be insulted.

"You thought I was going to say something like a mighty German shepherd? Some valiant breed of dog?"

"I was hoping...."

Giggling, Wild Woman said, "Ask me why I said bloodhound. Go on, ask me."

Mace felt his lips pulling into a smile as she relentlessly teased him. Yes, she was baiting him, but she wasn't mean. He doubted if she had a nasty bone in her body. Unlike him.

Touching the skin under his eyes, he murmured, "My bags?"

Jessica threw her head back and howled. When Mace joined in, the sound was like the resonate beat of a drum. The special drum used in a sweat lodge, which literally moved sound waves through participants to engage their spirit. Mace's laugh was like that. It rocked her world.

Wiping tears of laughter from her cheeks, Jessie said, "You certainly do *not* have bags under your eyes, Mace! Far from it." She saw the humor dancing in his green eyes. "I like you like this. You ought to get drunk more often, let down your hair and be a tad silly like me."

"I'm taking lessons from the master, for sure."

She snickered. "Touché, maestro. Touché."

"Come on, why a bloodhound of all dogs?"

"Well, for one thing, they're trained trackers.

Damn good at it, too. Once they're on a scent, they don't lose it. Aren't you like that?"

"I...guess so."

"It was a compliment!"

"Okay... I'm a tracker. Is that all?"

"No," Jessica whispered, "that's not all, Mace. A bloodhound has a sad face. And sadness surrounds you like a heavy, dark cloud...."

Mace felt as if someone had unexpectedly stabbed him in the heart with a knife. He felt the pain go all the way to his soul. His brows fell. His mouth twisted inward. His fingers tightened around the glass until he thought he might snap the stem in half. Jessie's voice was so gentle and nurturing that he couldn't raise any defense against her.

He sat in the chair, feeling helpless. As if she'd peeled back all of his armor, leaving him feeling horribly naked and vulnerable. At the same time, as Mace turned his head and held her soft blue gaze, those lips of hers parted, and her care blanketed him. Now he saw why she was on this mission. She thought on her feet. She was clever. She could outwit others. She'd boxed him in with words as adroitly as a fighter maneuvered another into the ropes.

"You have damn good insight into people."

"I try never to use it against them," Jessie said in a hushed tone, watching the color drain from his face. "I try to understand why people are the way they are."

Sensing an opening, Wild Woman relied solely on her intuition. She understood that, more than anything, she must get to the heart of Mace. He was a stranger to her, and yet in less than twelve hours they were going to put their lives on the line together and she needed to understand him. Trust had to be built as swiftly as possible between them. And to her, that could be achieved only by revealing their true selves to each other. No lies. No shields. Just honesty.

"Why so sad, Mace? What happened to you?"

Mace didn't know why; he just knew in his gut that it was important to share with Jessie. With a sigh, he began. "I married Jillian when I was eighteen years old. I'd had a crush on her all through high school. Our parents weren't very happy about it, but we loved each other so much that we knew we could make it work.

"We put off having children until we finished college. Jillian got her degree in social work, and I got one in criminology. I joined the Marine Corps and went into recon. Jillian practiced wherever I was assigned."

Pain began to suffuse him. His heart felt raw. "I was in South America on a black ops when I was told that I was receiving emergency leave."

Frowning, Jessie leaned forward. "Why?" She held her breath, seeing the devastation in his eyes.

"Jillian had just found out that she had a rare, aggressive form of ovarian cancer. I came home the same day they were taking her into surgery to re-move everything."

"I'm so sorry…." Jessica whispered.

"I don't know who cried more when she came out of the operation. Jillian cried for the kids she couldn't have. I cried for her because the surgeon told us the cancer had already spread throughout her lymph system. Even with aggressive chemo and ra-diation, Jillian had, at most, six months to live."

"I see…." The suffering was exquisite on his fea-tures. Her own heart breaking for him, Jessie reached out and rested her hand on his hunched shoulder. Even beneath his blazer she could feel the tension in his muscles.

"I'm not going to go into the next four months," Mace said. "Jillian refused chemo and radiation. She felt the treatments would only end her life more quickly and she'd suffer even more. She knew she was going to die and she wanted quality time with me. I agreed with her."

"You had four months?"

"Believe me, we counted every day. I tried not to show my heartbreak…but on more days than not, we'd fall into one another's arms, crying."

Jessie squeezed his shoulder before she removed her hand. "Oh, Mace, tears are good. I'm sure releas-ing all your grief, your anger and hopelessness was a good thing, not a bad one."

Shaking his head, he looked at her ruefully. "You know, Jillian said the same thing, almost word for word, to me."

"And after she died, what did you do?" Jessie knew the healing quality of being able to speak to someone of such a grievous wound. Clearly, Mace still suffered from it. She saw a glimmer in his eyes, and although he refused to look at her, she sensed it was from tears he stubbornly refused to let fall.

"Got lost. I took thirty days leave and backpacked into the Sierras. I was alone. I cried endlessly. I felt abandoned. I missed Jillian so much…." Mace missed the warm contact of Jessie's hand on his shoulder. And if he was honest, right now all he wanted to do was crawl into her arms. The tender compassion in her blue eyes, the tears that swam in them, touched him as nothing else had since his loss of Jillian.

Clearing his throat, he clasped his hands in his lap. "I had one year left in the corps. I was so torn up by the loss of my wife that I was barely functioning. Lucky for me, my commander put me on a desk job at Camp Reed in California, where I couldn't screw anything up." Mace felt the heat of tears burning in his eyes. "I owe him a lot. I could have hurt my recon team, given the emotional shape I was in, and he knew it. Instead, he encouraged me to pursue the CIA because of my linguistics background.

I think the only thing that saved me was taking Chinese classes three nights a week at the university nearby. I was able to funnel my grief into work."

"Friends can make all the difference," Jessie whispered, her voice catching. Wiping her eyes, she said, "No wonder you're so sad...."

"Enough time has gone by that I don't feel like I'll go crazy. Maybe I needed these three months in a lead-lined room. I don't know...."

Reaching out, Jessie ran her fingers gently across his short, dark hair. "You did what you had to do to survive losing the love of a lifetime, Mace. I'd give anything to meet a man that I love as much as you loved your Jillian. You were so blessed."

Her understanding was blinding. Healing. "We *were* blessed. And you're right, not many people will ever experience the kind of love we had. Even if I lost it too soon, I know what real love is."

Jessie gripped his shoulder. "Don't be that sad bloodhound. Don't give up on life, Mace, because I see life in you. But I feel like you're just going through the motions, not really living."

He managed an abrupt laugh. "It's hell living, Jessie. It's damn painful."

"And because it is, you've decided to barricade yourself behind a big, thick wall. What you can't feel can't hurt you. I know the attitude. I've seen it before. But you know what? Living like that is living a lie. We weren't put down here not to feel, not to cry, not to love, to experience joy and the ups and downs that life throws at us. At some point, you're going to have to break down your walls and *feel* again."

Chapter 5

She was right. Mace looked down at the carpeted deck, the pain consuming him. A lump formed in his throat and he swallowed several times to get rid of it. It was a lump of grief that had remained stubbornly stuck for so long because he'd been unable to cry out the last of his loss. To howl out his grief and loss. Yet Jessie had been able to trigger tears in his eyes as effortlessly as a rainbow was created after the rain.

Mace lifted his head. He wasn't prepared for the tears tracking down her own cheeks, her blue eyes tender with...what? He couldn't decipher the emotion except that it was for him. Instantly, his heart rebounded. Some of the agony that had held it in such an unrelenting vise began to dissolve. That in itself was a miracle, Mace decided. Self-consciously, he fumbled in his back pocket for his white linen handkerchief and handed it to her.

"Here," he muttered, "you need this...."

"Thanks, Mace." She took the proffered linen from his hand. Blotting her eyes, she gave him a trembling smile. "That is such a sad, sad story. No wonder I felt that heaviness around you. I'm sorry I made you relive it. I just thought...well, I didn't think. I hope you forgive me?"

He nodded. "There's nothing to forgive. We're going to be working very closely together. And where we're going, we'll need to communicate with one another...and to trust."

Returning the damp handkerchief, Jessie said, "That's why I did it. I didn't understand the darkness around you. I wanted to find out who the *real* Mace was. Now I know."

"I'm a lot better than I used to be," he murmured wryly, tucking the handkerchief into the back pocket of his slacks.

Jessie sat back in her roomy seat and sighed. "I've never lost someone I love. At least...not yet. Oh, I worry every day we fly combat missions in Peru. I worry for my girlfriends—that they'll get shot out of the sky by a sneaky Black Shark. But so far, I haven't lost someone dear to me...."

"It's not something I'd wish on anyone." Mace gazed over at Jessie. The black wig she wore for her cover only enhanced her lovely face, her high cheekbones. He found himself looking hungrily at her soft, parted lips. What would it be like to touch Jessie there? Taste her? Every woman, Mace knew, had a unique flavor. Would she taste like honey? The dew from a flower? Though Jessie was up front and in his face, he'd seen her tender side and it drew him sharply. He saw yearning in her eyes, too. For him? Was he a fool to think that? What would that mean to their mission?

Mace had a helluva lot of questions and no answers, and he cautioned himself to go slow. Find out who *she* was. Create that trust that could well save their lives if they got into dire straits with Robert Marston in Hong Kong.

"Enough about me. What about you, Jessie? Tell me more about yourself. Your growing up years. How you got into army aviation." Most of all, Mace wanted to know if she had a significant other. There had been no ring on her left hand before they began the mission, but that meant nothing. He knew combat aviators never wore any jewelry; it was against regulations. For this undercover assignment, however, Jessie wore a wedding ring—a diamond.

"Me? Oh, dude, you do not have the time to hear of my wild upbringing on the res!"

Looking at the gold Rolex on his right wrist, he said, "According to my watch, you and I still have plenty of time on this flight to do just that. I'm listening."

Seeing the earnestness in his eyes, Jessie sighed and said, "Okay. It's important we know something of one another before we get to the Hong Kong airport. The moment we step off this plane, we have to be a happily married couple."

Boarding the plane, they'd hammed it up, acting like a couple in love for the benefit of the flight crew. Jessie had enjoyed holding Mace's hand, hanging on to him as a wife would her husband. But after reaching their seats in the jumbo jet, they'd allowed that facade to quickly drop away. Although they suspected there were no spies on board the flight, by being in the hump, alone, they were saved from any possible prying eyes.

"Okay, about me… Well, like I said, I grew up in Lame Deer, Montana, on the Northern Cheyenne Reservation. It's a small res, about fifty-five square miles. About two thousand of us lived there. My mother was born in Lame Deer, grew up there, and my parents still live there now. My mom is one of the medicine women on the res, and her mission is healing and helping others.

"Let's see, after we moved back from Texas I finished my last two years at Lame Deer High School. From there, I went to Montana State University in Bozeman for three years and then quit."

"Why did you quit?"

"I got bored. I'm one of those people that don't like to read about adventure, but want to go out and *live* it. I was working toward a degree in aeronautical engineering when I left Montana State."

"So you loved to fly?"

"It was in my heart and soul, Mace. My father had been a U.S. Navy SEAL. He was a licensed small-plane pilot when I was growing up, and I got my love of flying from him. I knew my parents would be devastated that I was quitting college to take a shot at being in the first all-woman class at Apache combat helicopter flight school, but I had to try."

"And did your parents support you?"

She chuckled. "Oh, yeah. My mother and father always told me I could do anything I wanted to do in life." She smiled wickedly. "And my mother, in particular, really pushed home the fact that I was a 'way shower' and could do anything I set my mind to. I believed that. I do to this day."

"It sounds like they gave you great personal support."

"They did. They still do." Jessica shifted in her seat, hanging her legs over the arm again, and faced

Mace. He looked less dark to her now. Maybe that was her intuition, or the gift of clairvoyance passed from mother to daughter. Sometimes, when she was relaxed or in danger, Jessie could see colors around people. She knew she was seeing their auras, something her mother had taught her early on to perceive. Right now, as she unfocused her eyes and looked beyond Mace, she saw that the gunmetal gray that had been around him was gone, replaced by pastel glimmers. That told her that their intense discussion had been helpful. She was glad, because Mace didn't deserve to suffer endlessly as he had. Smiling to herself, Jessie decided that maybe she had a little more of her mother's healing talents than she'd thought. Mace had responded to her care and concern. That touched her deeply.

"And so you made history by being a graduate of Fort Rucker and flying the Apache helicopter?" Mace said, interrupting her thoughts.

"Yep." She lifted her empty champagne glass in a mock toast. "It was hell getting through because the C.O. didn't want women in the seat of a combat helicopter. His name was Captain Dane York, and he hated us. Because of his prejudice, some of the upper classmen saw that as permission to mess with us. Snake damn near got done in." Jessie shrugged. "We were in combat the moment we entered flight school. After we graduated, we went directly into combat of a different kind in Peru. I've been there ever since...until now." She smiled. "And I have to admit, this is a helluva lot more fun so far."

"You needed a break from the tension and demands."

Jessie was glad he understood. Mace was very quick to grasp a situation and size it up. That made him a good agent. "Yes, you're right. To me, this is a real vacation. And not only that, I have a damn good-lookin' dude workin' with me. If my compadres in Peru knew what I had going here, they'd be green with envy," she said, laughing.

Heat crept up Mace's neck. He was flushing—again. Looking away, he savored the feelings that came with her admission. "I've never thought of myself as handsome."

Jessie reached over and playfully struck him on the shoulder. "Oh, come on! You are! You look more like a magazine cover model than a stoic ole CIA agent!"

An unwilling grin pulled at the corners of his mouth. "Are you always playing?"

Shrugging, Jessie said, "I don't like the other choice—being too damn serious all the time. Do you?"

"I've always been serious, even as a child."

"That's what the firstborn gets for his trouble of arriving at the head of the line in a family." She laughed again.

"You aren't like this in the cockpit, are you?"

"Anytime I can get away with it, I am."

Looking into Jessie's dancing blue eyes, Mace said, "But when it comes down to the business of business?" He watched her eyes narrow and become coolly thoughtful.

"I've stared death in the face more times than I can count. And won. I don't know if you know anything about Cheyenne Dog Soldiers, but they were the cream of the crop among our nation's warriors. My mother's side boasted Dog Soldiers and medicine people. All the women were warriors by bloodline and tradition. Even though some went into training to become healers, many fought for our nation against the Crow, the Flatheads, Blackfeet and others—and were victorious." Jessie leaned closer. "I'm a war woman, Mace. The blood of the Dog Soldiers runs in my veins and I'm very good at what I do. A Dog Soldier's job is to protect the village and the people in it. In Peru, I see myself as protecting the world from the devastation of cocaine. We stop the flights. We turn them back. Every time we take to the air, we're at war with the mercenaries flying those Black Shark helicopters. No, Mace, when it comes down to getting the job done, I don't play around. That's the time the Dog Soldier rises in me and I'm all-business. And I'm not in the habit of losing."

There was a side to Jessica Merrill that many women did not possess, and, God help him, it drew him powerfully. Mace liked strong women. He'd been married to one. And Jessica was a true warrior through blood and heritage, as well as her training as a combat helicopter pilot.

"Tell me more about your father. What did he do after he retired from the navy?"

"Oh, Dad! Well!" Jessie leaned back in the seat and gave him that wolfish smile of hers. "He put in his twenty in the navy and was a damn good SEAL. After that, he met my mother, got married and went into law enforcement on her reservation. We moved to Texas when I was six years old. Right now, he's the chief of police in Lame Deer." She laughed as memories seemed to flood her. "From the earliest I can remember, he's always challenged me to put jig-saw puzzles together. He taught me to play chess when I was eight years old. For him, it was impor-tant that I think with strategy and tactics, and I do."

"I suppose he gave you a Rubic's Cube and you decimated it in two minutes flat?"

"One minute fifty seconds. My dad timed me."

"Amazing."

"Like I said, I'm a pretty amazing woman," she said, laughing heartily.

"So he taught you how to think in a clever way."

"Oh, more than that! He taught me how to pick

locks, read people and know how to get around them to get what I want." She held up her hand as if to stop an objection from him. "Now, in my dad's job as a SEAL, his life depended upon how he read a situation or a person…or picked a lock. He got very good at it."

"Maybe your dad's teaching will serve us well on this mission. We might have to pick a couple of locks."

"I know," she said, nodding her head. "And I brought my set of picks along—just in case." She winked at him.

"Why do I think I've just been teamed up with Mata Hari?"

"Oh, because you have been, Mr. CIA Agent." She buffed her short nails against her magenta silk tank top and looked at them.

Mace's heart beat a little harder. He had to ask the ten million dollar question he was dying to know the answer to. "Is there anyone in your life in Peru?"

"Just the girls," Wild Woman answered.

"There's got to be a city nearby where you can get some R and R? Let down your wild blond, red-streaked hair?"

She grinned. "Oh, yeah. Cuzco. Me and Snake go there every chance we get and tango with the good-lookin' Latin dudes. We drink pisco, a local liquor that will kick the slats out from under you in a heartbeat, and dance until they close the place down. It sure sheds the tension of the job."

"Are you serious with any of these Latin dudes?"

Shaking her head, Jessie said, "Listen, in our business you can't tell anyone who you really are. Snake and I go incognito. We usually pretended to be *turistas* from Argentina or some other country. We speak Spanish and have the same skin coloring. Snake is half Navajo and even more Indian looking than me. So the guys believe us and the stories we concoct." She tugged at one of her long black braids and smiled. "We wear wigs, too."

"Obviously, you have a lot of practice at this." Mace marveled again at her intelligence and savvy.

Wild Woman sighed dramatically. "Under the circumstances, I couldn't meet Mr. Right if I tried. When you're in a black ops, you're limited. Besides, the BJS was an all-woman operation until very recently. There are a few male pilots now." She shrugged. "None of them interest me."

"What kind of man does interest you?" There, it was out of his mouth. Mace was shocked at his own nervy question. Jessie's eyes had a look of pure wickedness. That sinful mouth of hers curved upward deliciously. If only he could lean over, brush his lips against hers and find out just how soft and silky she was...

"Ah...significant others. Now there's the point of the spear, isn't it?"

"I don't know. Is it?"

"I like men. I really do. But you know what? Most of them aren't worth the price of admission. Don't take this the wrong way. I'm really spoiled. My dad is to blame, really. Even though he's a warrior, he has something else most men simply do not possess—a woman's energy.

"Native Americans know that within each male is the energy of the female—and vice versa. If a man is genuinely working to become whole and in harmony, he allows the feminine energy within him to integrate and express itself, along with his masculine energy. And if that happens, the man may be Mr. Testosterone when he needs to be, but when he doesn't, he can be as nurturing and emotionally expressive as any woman."

Struggling to understand her and compare himself to her ideal, Mace said, "So, your dad is..."

"My dad is strong and forthright when he needs to be. With my mother and me, he's tender, nurturing, protective and supportive. He knows how to cry, Mace. I've *seen* him cry a number of times. If a man is in harmony, he *can* cry and he understands there is no shame attached to it. Women cry all the time and never think a thing of it! We know it's better out than in. But Anglo males in North America...well, they don't know how to show their feelings, to be okay with their tears and to share them with those they love." She snorted and gave him a dark look. "Most white American guys are repressed to the point where I won't have a thing to do with them."

"I see…. So who would be your ideal mate then? What would he be like?"

"Strong. Protective. Nurturing. He could cry with me. He could laugh with me. He could let down his hair and be a kid. I've told you, I like to play, Mace! I love life. I want the man I fall in love with to be just as fierce at loving and living life as I am. I want to know that when he's at my side, he's there for me a hundred and ten percent. Just as I will be for him."

"Sounds like a tall order to fill."

"It is." Jessie laughed derisively. "That's why I don't have a significant other. I haven't found a man yet who can be tender like my dad. Open emotionally. Able to really, honest-to-God communicate at every level with me." She shrugged. "So, until then, I window-shop. When I can play with a guy, I go dancing, have a few drinks, let it all hang out and then go back home alone. Most men, I've found, are very shallow. They're afraid of commitment. They're afraid, period! And I don't want a partner who's emotionally afraid of me, my life, or what we might have if we came together."

Mace absorbed her impassioned declaration. He saw the seriousness in Jessie's eyes and heard it in her low, husky voice. She'd meant every word. And he wasn't sure if he met her requirements. Disappointment threaded through him.

"I play for keeps, Mace. I'm not into the let's-hop-into-bed-and-have-sex mentality. Oh, I can have fun with a guy. I love to dance. But unfortunately, most men see me as a piece of meat to be lured into bed and then left the next morning. I don't play that game. Never did and I'm not starting now."

"On that point, we agree. Sex is something that should come later in the relationship. It's a gift. One of the most beautiful a man can share with a woman. You're right, guys play too many games to get a woman into bed."

"My heart be still," she said dramatically, pressing her hand against her chest. "A man who agrees with me. Hey, Mace, you're looking better all the time. Keep it up!"

A snort of bashful laughter escaped him. Shaking his head, he said, "No, I don't even begin to meet your criteria, Jessie. I'm just one of those wounded white males slogging through each day wondering how he's going to survive to the next one."

"Oh, gimme a break!" Wild Woman muttered. "That's not true, Mace. Look what you just did—you talked to me about your life, what was important to you. You didn't avoid me. On the contrary, you look *real* good to me."

Hope suffused him, pushing the disappointment away. Mace realized that Jessie never questioned if he was interested in her or not. She already knew, somehow, that he was. How *did* she know? He hadn't been obvious at all…he thought. Yet, meeting her dancing gaze, he wondered how he could *not* want to have a relationship with this warrior woman.

Chapter 6

Jessie got her first glimpse of China through the windows of Hong Kong International Airport once they finally got out of customs and the baggage claim area. In the airy concourse of the busy airport she saw people of all nations, all colors and all garb. Mace had told her that Hong Kong, after reverting to Chinese control in 1997, remained one of the biggest business centers in the world. As she and Mace walked arm in arm toward a man holding a sign that read Mr. and Mrs. Creighton Webb, she was awed by the flurry of activity around them.

She knew the man waiting for them in a trim

black uniform was a limousine driver from the Shangri-La Hotel, where they were going to stay. The man held up a sign with their last name on it. Might as well look happily married! Smiling up at Mace, Jessie found it easy to pretend that he really was her husband. Quickly standing on tiptoe, she planted a warm kiss on Mace's recently shaved cheek. She saw the surprise in his eyes when she whispered, "All's fair in love and war, darling."

A slow smile crawled across his mouth. "I think you're enjoying this, Mrs. Webb."

"Oh, I am, I am, Mr. Webb. More than you'll ever know!"

His cheek tingled where she'd placed her soft mouth against his flesh. Too bad he hadn't seen it coming; he'd have turned and met her mouth with his. Well, forewarned was forearmed. She was obviously into the drama of her part. He could be, too.

Turning his attention to the tall, lean Chinese man with scrupulously arranged short black hair, dark framed glasses and a neat mustache above his wide, smiling mouth, Mace said, "Mr. Kang? I'm Creighton Webb. This is my lovely wife, Jessica." The name of their driver was written on their travel itinerary.

Bowing deeply, Mr. Kang said in flawless English, "Welcome to Hong Kong, sir and madam. Please allow my assistant to load your luggage in the car."

Mace handed over their baggage. "Excellent."

Kang bowed again. Smiling, he said, "Please, follow me."

Jessica could smell the salt in the air as they exited the architectural wonder that was the airport. Nearby was the gray-green water of Victoria Harbour. The sky was a misty blue streaked with white cirrus clouds. The sun was warm, the breeze delightful and invigorating after the recirculated air in the jumbo jet.

When they reached the back door of a silver Rolls Royce, Kang opened it and gestured for her to step in. Ah! So this was what it felt like to be filthy rich! The plush leather seats were incredibly soft, Jessie discovered as she slid into the limousine. Mace followed. Kang shut the door and they were off.

Eyes wide, Jessica said nothing but looked endlessly out the windows as the Rolls glided smoothly through the maze of heavy traffic. She saw a few junks sailing in the harbor, Chinese men pedaling rickshaws loaded with tourists, and more bicycle riders than she could ever count.

"What a busy, busy place..." Jessie said, smiling when Mace slid his hand into hers and placed their joined hands on his hard thigh. That was more like it!

Reviewing the small map that Mace had given her, she realized that the airport was located on a tiny island far from Hong Kong. They would have to drive through a tunnel under the sea to Lantau Island. From there, another tunnel would bring them to Tsing Yi, where they would take a third tunnel to Kowloon, their final destination. It was a heck of a drive, in Jessie's opinion. A long one.

"Next time," she said, leaning close to Mace so her lips were near his ear, "how about a quick helicopter flight from the airport to the hotel helipad?"

Smiling, Mace squeezed her hand. He liked that she squeezed his in return. As she rested her chin on his shoulder, her lips so close, he placed a soft kiss on her cheek. She smelled like wildflowers.

Getting a grip on his escalating desire, he said, "That was an option, Mrs. Webb, but since this is your first trip here, I thought you might like to see the country firsthand, catch a bit of the flavor."

Mace wouldn't put it past Marston to bug the Rolls. And he wasn't about to blow their cover. Kang, who was watching them off and on in the rearview mirror, understood English very well, Mace knew.

"Well, darling, this is exciting and all, but you know me. I love to fly." Jessie gave him her best pout. "And I can hardly wait to fly our Titan helicopter."

"All things in good time, luv." He smiled down into her eyes, feeling the warmth of her hand as she slid it slowly and provocatively up his arm. This woman was going to drive him crazy with longing.

Jessie was thrilled with their penthouse digs at the Shangri-La Hotel. By the time they were admitted to their room, their luggage had been opened and their clothes put away in the Louis XV dressers. The first thing Mace did when the bellman left them alone was put his fingers to his lips. Nodding, Jessie knew what he was going to do: look for bugs. Her father had taught her about listening devices, and she started her own search in one of the two suites that comprised the spacious penthouse.

"Oh, darling, I am so tired," Jessie said, examining the lamps, checking under them and around each table they sat on.

"I am, too, luv," Mace called from the far side of the room. They kept up their patter as they scoured the entire area.

After a thirty-minute search, Mace pulled Jessie to his side. "I don't see anything."

A sudden thought hit Jessie. She gripped his hand and pulled him toward the sliding mirrored doors where their luggage had been stored. Opening the closet, she said, "Darling, I think they left my comb and brush in our bags. Would you please go look for them?"

"Of course," he answered, hauling out all four pieces of their Luis Vuitton luggage and throwing them on the king-size bed.

Jessica stood back, watching how thorough and quick Mace was with his search. She liked his hands; they were long, lean, with dark hair on top. She saw Mace frown and her heart stopped for a moment as he slid his fingers deeper into one pocket of the luggage. Jessie moved closer and she saw him pull out a small, round metal device.

Mace scowled. Damn. It was a bug. That meant that Marston was already investigating them. The dossier on the billionaire had provided ample evidence that Marston routinely "bugged" his guests. Because he was paranoid? A powermonger who felt he had the right to invade the privacy of whomever he pleased? Mace didn't know, but he was glad he had checked for the devices. He showed the bug to Jessie before carefully placing it back in the luggage.

"Ah, here's your comb and brush, luv."

"Thanks. I just *have* to take a hot shower, wash my hair and get this airplane filth off me. Ugh!"

After storing the luggage back in the closet, Mace pulled Jessie into the massive marble bathroom and closed the door. He made a cursory inspection of the room even though he'd gone over it once already. If there was one bug, there could sure as hell be more...

He turned on the shower full force and took Jessie's hand, pulling her close to him and absorbing her softness. "We have to be careful where and when we talk, Jessie. We've searched this place, but they could have bugs so fine and hard to see that we have to assume someone is listening to everything we say."

"I understand."

"Have your shower, okay? I'm going to do a little reconnoitering around the place."

"Okay. I'll get cleaned up. I'm tired, Mace. Can we knock off for some sleep?"

He squeezed her briefly. "You bet." He saw the glimmer in her eyes. "You okay sleeping with me?"

"That's the easy part," she said breathily. "And I really *like* holding your hand and kissing you when you least expect it."

Giving her a long, burning look, Mace said, "If I didn't know better, I'd say you're flirting with me, Wild Woman." When her lips curved into a huge smile, he found himself smiling in return.

"This is the *best* part of the trip as far as I'm concerned." She touched his chest, laying her hand over his heart. "And I hope you aren't uncomfortable with my flirting? Because if you are, say so."

"I like your brazenness. And your honesty. You're not going to hear me protest."

Laughing softly, Jessie eased away. "Okay, get out of here...or I'm going to go naked on you, fella."

Now was that an invitation or not? He wasn't sure

how serious Jessie was about him, or if she was simply playing the make-believe game that she was so good at in Peru. Lifting his hand in farewell, he left the bathroom.

When Mace returned from his walk around the hotel, Jessie had already thrown back the covers on the king-size bed.

"Hey, you getting ready to crash?" he asked from the doorway, hands on his hips. How delicious Jessie looked. She'd unbound the braids of her wig so that hair fell around her proud shoulders. He watched as she quickly gathered the thick, long strands into a ponytail. Beneath a lavender silk bathrobe that fell to her ankles, she wore a loose-fitting violet tank top and a pair of boxer shorts. The outfit showed off her trim body to decided advantage.

"More than ready. That hot shower felled me, Mace."

"I won't be far behind," he said. "I'll join you shortly." Yeah, that was a heated idea, for sure.

She winked at him. "I'll be waiting."

Mace entered the bathroom and readied the shower, all the while feeling like a kid in a candy store, with Jessie the candy. Excitement thrummed through him as he scrubbed off a day's worth of airline traveling. Being rich meant getting the royal treatment. No detail had been overlooked, that was for sure.

The French-milled soap provided for male guests had a spicy lime fragrance. The soap for the women staying in the penthouse was a lavender color and smelled lightly of lilacs.

As Mace scrubbed his hair with a mango-scented shampoo, his thoughts swung back to Jessie. They would have to sleep in the same bed—together. Although he hadn't found any cameras on the premises, for safety's sake, to protect their cover, he had to sleep with her. Not that he didn't want to. He wanted to real bad. He knew Jessie would be a wild lover—hot, sweet, spicy and sexy. But was he ready for that?

He'd courted Jillian for years and never touched her. And all he wanted to do now was touch Jessie and never stop. What the hell was he going to do? What if she made the first advance? Say stop? He wanted her, that was for damn sure. But for all the wrong reasons. He'd gone years without sex. His grief had kept him from even thinking about it since Jillian's death. Until now.

Groaning softly, Mace shut off the shower and stepped out. Grabbing a lush pink towel, he scrubbed his hair until it was almost dry. The crinkly sensation of the lamb's wool mat beneath his feet made him only more aware of how sensitive he was right now. And it had to be because of Jessie. Somehow she'd triggered his will to live again. How she'd done it was beyond him. He was just a white American male who didn't have a clue, as she would say. Smiling a little, he hung the damp towel on the fourteen-carat-gold rack and grabbed a dry white one to tie at his waist before going to the basin to brush his teeth. What *was* he going to do? How was he going to keep his hands off Jessie? The thoughts assailed him as he brushed and rinsed and, later, as he changed into his pajama bottoms in their bedroom.

When Mace finally approached their bed with its pristine white silk duvet, he saw that Jessie was sound asleep. She lay on her stomach, her head turned to one side, her hand near her lips. She looked angelic and small in the huge bed.

Standing beside it, Mace felt so many emotions begin to awaken in him. He saw that one of the tank top's spaghetti straps had snagged against Jessie's upper arm. She was in such good shape, her flesh so firm.

Her lips were parted. Mace could hear her breath moving in and out, in and out. So soft. So…heavenly in a way. How he'd missed Jillian's warmth at his side all these lonely nights of hell. He missed her breath against his neck or shoulder, her arm stretched languidly across his body.

Swallowing hard, he carefully pulled the duvet down and moved the sheet aside. There was no way they could cheat in this undercover game. His mind

spun with possible scenarios. What if the butler unexpectedly came into the room? That could happen.
Or their personal chef? Or who knew who else from
the hotel staff? If Mace slept apart from her, tongues
would wag. No, he had to climb into bed and snug-
gle up to Jessie, no matter how scared he was.

Scared? Yeah, friggin' scared up to his eyeballs.

But was he more afraid of her or of himself? Well,
he was about to find out.

Chapter 7

The sensation of a man, his arm wrapped around her as she pressed against the hard length of his body, entered Jessie's waking consciousness. Thinking it was a sinfully delicious dream, she burrowed even more deeply into the warm shoulder where her head rested, her nose against his throat, her brow against his sandpapery jaw. Her arm rested across his torso, and she could feel the smooth, even breathing that told her he was sleeping deeply.

Suddenly, her drowsy mind, which was still pulling out of that dark whirlpool of sleep, cautioned, *No, this is real. This is not a dream.*

Her lashes lifted. Jessie lay very still, evaluating her position. She saw that the sumptuous white brocade drapes had been drawn shut, but a slight gap revealed that it was nighttime. That would be right. They'd left on the red-eye from Seattle and arrived at 10:00 a.m. in China the next day. And she'd gone to bed around noon. Playing with the math in her head stopped abruptly as Jessie realized it was Mace who she was snuggled against. How many hours she'd slept wasn't important now—where she was lying was.

Mace was naked except for a pair of cotton pajama bottoms. She had to admit to herself that she liked the springy hair that her fingers grazed as she slowly pulled her arm free of his narrow waist. Rubbing her eyes, she remained on her side, pressed up against him. Absorbing the sound of his breathing, she eased her head back just enough to look at his shadowed profile. Smiling, she understood that in sleep Mace was not in pain or suffering. She was glad for him.

Beneath the covers her knee lay across Mace's leg. He was very strong. She knew he worked out regularly by the feel of his hardened thigh beneath hers. It was such a luxury to be awake just enough to appreciate his warm maleness. Most of all, Jessie liked the fact that he was holding her. That sensation became indelibly etched upon her heart.

The scent of him entered her flaring nostrils as she eased back down against him, resting her brow against his jaw once again. The masculine fragrance was an aphrodisiac to her. She carefully laid her arm across his torso once more, not wanting to wake him. She knew it was probably the wee hours before dawn. They wouldn't be awakened by the butler until 8:00 a.m., so Jessie closed her eyes and snuggled close once more.

How long had it been since she'd lain with a man? Four years? Oh, that was far too long! But being part of BJS denied her a true relationship with a man. At least, a serious one in which she could share herself with him, share a bed with him, was out of the question. It was one thing to go to town and dance, get drunk and party in Cuzco with the local guys; it was quite another to allow friendly kisses to turn into lovemaking.

Well, this time with Mace was a gift, Jessie decided. As she allowed herself to spiral into a deep sleep once again, she understood that he wasn't ready for a red-hot relationship. She'd seen his lingering grief over the loss of his beloved wife, and she respected that. In her heart, Jessie wanted Mace to come to her, to lie with her out on a grassy slope in the sunlight and make love with her. Was that possible? She didn't know. She *did* know that he was drawn to her.

Well, she would do what she could to draw him
out of the past and remind him that living life was a
beautiful thing. Of course, that left her in a very
risky emotional position. As she extended the olive
branch of life to him, her heart, her feelings were also being given. If anything, Jessie was a realist; she
knew he could reject her completely. Still, she had
these precious days in Hong Kong to launch a sweet
assault upon him, reminding him that life was worth
sinking his teeth into and, maybe, that she was a wor-
thy partner.

Maybe…

A sharp knock jerked Jessie from her sleep. Sitting up, groggy and disoriented, she looked around.

"I'll get it," Mace told her quietly, holding up his
hand to stay her as he walked to the marble foyer.

Confused, Jessie remained in bed, scrubbing her
eyes, her legs crossed beneath the sheet. What time
was it? She could hear Mace talking to the butler.
Soon, he returned to their bedroom, wheeling a table filled with breakfast, a crystal vase of red roses
in the center.

Jessie could see that he'd recently showered; his
black hair damp and gleaming with blue highlights.
He'd shaved, too, and was dressed in dark gray
slacks, a pale pink, short-sleeved shirt with a white
T-shirt beneath it.

"Gawd...what time is it?" she muttered thickly, trying to wake up.

"Eight o'clock, darling. Come on, throw on a robe and join me for what looks to be a great breakfast." Mace couldn't take his eyes from Jessie. Her wig had slipped off during the night, leaving her blond hair with the red streak looking like a little girl's mussed hairdo. On her, the look was priceless and fetching. As she ran her fingers through her hair, she realized that the wig was gone and started to panic.

"It's on the dresser," he told her, carrying two gilded chairs with white brocade seats to the linen-covered table.

"Oh!" She pressed her hand to her pounding heart. "It must have..."

"Yeah." Mace smiled. How beautiful Jessie looked! "Come on, your robe's at the end of the bed."

Jessie sprang out of bed, grabbed her silk robe and hurried to the bathroom. "I'll be back in a sec. Pour me coffee?"

"You bet."

Finishing her toilet, Jessie decided to leave the wig where it lay, and hurried to the table. As she approached, Mace got up and walked around the table to slide the chair out for her.

"Thanks."

"Coffee's in front of you."

"Thank you, Great Spirit!" she whispered, lifting the white china cup trimmed with gold. Taking a sip, she tipped her head back, closed her eyes and said, "Mmm…nectar of the goddesses. Thank you, Mace."

Chuckling, he removed the silver dome from her plate. "Here's breakfast, darling. I hope you're hungry."

The smell of cooked bacon made her mouth water as Mace set the metal dome aside. Her plate was filled with freshly scrambled eggs, a rasher of bacon, whole wheat toast and a small jar of salsa on the side. She liked hot, spicy salsa on her eggs. *Huevos rancheros,* a Mexican breakfast favorite, was something that had stuck with her since the time when her parents moved to Texas for a while. Opening the jar of salsa, Jessie quickly spread it over her fluffy scrambled eggs. She lifted her head and saw Mace watching her, a grin on his mouth. A mouth she could have kissed last night—wanted to kiss—but hadn't out of respect for him.

"What?" she demanded archly, closing the lid and setting the salsa aside.

"That's pretty hot stuff."

"I know. It's the way I like my eggs."

"Hot and fiery. Phew." Shaking his head, Mace cut into his two eggs, which had been prepared over easy.

Realizing he was teasing her, Jessie smiled and scooped up eggs onto her fork. "I was dead to the world."

"You were sawing logs."

Snorting softly, she forked the eggs into her mouth. They were warm and delicious. "Sawing logs?"

"Yeah, you know, snoring."

"Oh, pul-lease!" Jessie laughed as she buttered her toast. She was hungry and decided that if she wasn't filled up on what was on her plate, she could always dip into the basket of Danish pastries, croissants and muffins in the center of the table.

Mace chuckled. "You slept well last night," he murmured between bites.

"So did you." Knowing she was blushing, she took great pleasure in seeing Mace's cheeks turn red as well. *Gotcha!*

"I woke up in the middle of the night," she informed him, slathering strawberry jam across her toast, "and you were sawing logs yourself." He hadn't been snoring, but she wanted to tease him. Amusement glimmered in his green eyes. The tension between them was palpable.

"I don't remember. Jet lag always nails me bigtime." He picked up a croissant and buttered it. Reaching for the honey dispenser, he murmured, "But now, I wished I'd been awake…."

"Yeah?" Her lower body flared to life with yearning. Oh, what would have happened if she'd wakened Mace? Judging from the mirth in his eyes, she had made a huge mistake in realizing that he wanted her—just as much as she wanted him.

"Oh, yeah." With the possibility of the room being bugged, Mace couldn't say a lot of things he wanted to. This would have to do for now. As he drizzled honey across his croissant, he thought about how she might react to him pouring the amber sweetness down the center of her body and then slowly licking it off her soft, firm flesh.

Mace was shocked at his own thoughts. It seemed that no matter what he did, what he looked at, what she wore, he was thinking of ways to undress Jessie, touch her, hold her and move his body against hers. His feelings were a helluva lot more alive than he'd ever realized. Or, he thought as he set the honey back down on the table, perhaps the right woman had only come along now to let him know that the winter of his grief was over and it was time to begin to live—and love—again.

Disgruntled, Mace bowed his head and focused on his food. Wild Woman was a damn good name for her. She'd crashed abruptly into his life like a proverbial bolt of lightning, awakening him to the fact that he was ready to take life on once more. Mace lifted his head to look at Jessie. Her hair was tousled and she looked excruciatingly beautiful this morning, her eyes slightly puffy from nearly twelve hours of sleep. Her bone structure reminded him of an ancient Egyptian statue of Nefertiti, the beautiful queen of Amenhotep IV. Merriment danced now in her sky-blue eyes and her quirky smile said, "Bring it on!"

"Why didn't you wake me up, then?" *To hell with it.* He *wanted* Jessie to know that he was interested in her. They might be only playing at being married, but Mace was ready to use their cover as an excuse to get as close as she'd allow him. And it was, after all, up to Jessie to define that closeness.

"Oh! And what would you have done if I'd awakened you with a kiss, I wonder?" Jessie knew someone could be listening. She had to be careful how she phrased things. They were supposed to have been married for five years. How did married people talk, anyway? She hadn't a clue! Picking up her glass of freshly squeezed orange juice, she sipped it and watched Mace lift his head. For the first time, he smiled. *Really* smiled.

"What do you think?"

Jessie gulped down the juice and set the glass back on the table, her breath hitching at this complete new side to Mace. No longer were his eyes dark with pain. They were such a clear green now that Jessie felt herself drawn into them. The genuine warmth of his smile curled around her heart, making it beat even faster. The energy around him changed dramatically, and again she felt embraced by it. There was a sense of being nurtured, protected and desired. The startling amount of feelings he was sending to her on a nonverbal level stunned her. They were such a priceless gift. Jessie stared at him as he reached across the table, took her hand for just a moment and squeezed it gently. She returned the squeeze.

"Well, next time I will wake you up and see where it all goes," she said.

Nodding, Mace held her gaze. "My warrior woman," he murmured. "The only place for you is in my arms. In *my* bed."

Shock riveted Jessie. Mace meant it. She saw it in the serious look he gave her despite his devastating smile.

"Game on," she purred.

"I read you loud and clear," Mace said, holding her gaze as he bit into the honeyed croissant.

She wanted to continue their heated exchange but business took priority. With a sigh, she asked, "What's on the agenda today?" Jessie pushed aside her plate and reached for one of the fragrant banana bran muffins.

"I got word from the butler that our helicopter has been delivered to the helipad on top of the hotel. I figured you'd like to fly us around the area. I can give you an air tour if you'll take the controls."

"I'd love to do that!" She split the muffin in half and bit into it.

"I thought you might. Once we get done with breakfast, we can sightsee, take some videos. I know how you like to have photos for your family."

Jessie nodded to acknowledge that she understood their hidden agenda. No doubt they'd be flying right over Marston's estate, taking plenty of photos that they could study at the hotel to get the lay of the land. "Oh, yes, my parents don't do much traveling, but they do love my digital photos. Let's spend a couple of hours in the air doing that, okay, darling?"

"All I want to do is make you happy," Mace told her. "I like seeing that smile in your eyes, luv."

She tingled at the huskily spoken endearment. "I can hardly wait to take off." Because then they could talk without any fear of bugs after they'd checked out the bird. And she had a helluva lot to pin him down on. Just how far did this make-believe marriage go? Seeing the desire burning in his eyes, Jessie didn't believe she could be reading Mace wrong.

The blue-and-silver helicopter was a dream to fly. Her hands around the cyclic and collective, Jessie guided the bird from the helipad toward the gray-green waters of Victoria Harbour nearby. The shaking and shuddering of the aircraft felt wonderful.

"I didn't know how *much* I'd miss flying until I couldn't just waltz out of my barracks and saddle up my Apache." She laughed and glanced over at Mace. Like her, he wore aviator glasses, a baseball cap and earphones.

"You fly like hot butter in a skillet," he said, smiling back at her. With her black braids hanging down over her dark red tank top, Jessie was spectacular looking. Today, she had on designer jeans and a pair of tennis shoes. Even though they were designer quality, she reminded him of the girl next door.

"Thanks. Flying is my passion."

You're my passion. Mace almost said the words aloud. He compressed his lips just in time. "You're a pro at this. I've flown in enough helicopters to know you have a light touch."

Below her, Wild Woman saw Hong Kong approaching. The island was on the opposite side of the harbor from Kowloon, where their hotel was located. On all sides of the S-shaped Victoria Harbour were now row after row of skyscrapers. She smiled. "Flying is like breathing. One and the same for me, Mace. What do you want to do first? Get photos of Marston's place? Do a little touring?" She glanced at the fuel gauge. "We've got five hundred pounds of fuel on board. We can stay airborne a couple of hours if you want."

Turning in his seat, Mace dug in the canvas bag he'd set behind it. Zipping it open, he pulled out a digital camera. "Let's mosey southeast, toward the end of the island, before heading to Aberdeen." He pointed toward the pyramid-shaped peak on Hong Kong island. "That's Victoria Peak. It's a great place to visit. Beautiful from the top. You look down over the city and harbor."

"I like the view from fifteen hundred feet, thank you very much."

Mace nodded in response as she fluidly eased the helicopter in the direction of Victoria Peak. Like the previous day, today was bright and beautiful, the sky a pale blue with wispy white clouds. Below them, she saw no waves on the South China Sea that would indicate wind disturbance. No, at 10:00 a.m. this part of China was peaceful and calm.

"It's amazing to see the many islands from the air!" Just yesterday, they'd driven from Hong Kong, which faced the New Territories on the Chinese mainland, to Kowloon. Jessie also spotted the larger Lantau Island. Mace had told her that there was a very old monastery there, Po Lin, which was considered very sacred to the Chinese people. All the islands were clothed in green. In this part of the world it rained most of the time, except in winter.

"There's a great botanical garden on the slopes of Victoria Peak. I'm hoping if we get the time, Jessie, we can go there. The flowers are knockouts, the orchids breathtaking."

Giving him a wry look, she said, "Speaking of breathtaking, Mace, I'm glad we're up here where no one can hear us. I got a lot of questions to ask you. Maybe we should have gone over these cover details beforehand, but I just didn't think about them, to tell you the truth."

"Sure, go ahead."

"First of all, how serious are you when you say all those delicious little things to me? Or give me those looks?"

"You mean where does the game end and reality begin?"

"Something like that." Guiding the helicopter over the peak, Jessie saw that it really wasn't that high and that a highway wound around it all the way to the top. There were cars parked all along the road and scores of people walking leisurely up and down the mountain.

"I'm not sure, if you want the truth. We're in a dead-serious game. We know someone is bugging us—more than likely Marston, but we don't know for sure. Staying in character as husband and wife…well, it's familiar to me, not to mention safe."

"Not to me. I've been single a long time. And I'm not quite sure how to read your come-on. Is it just a fake game to convince others we're in love or what?"

Mace was uncomfortable. Jessica shot straight from the hip with no diplomatic words. "I—don't know."

"But you like me?"

"Yes, I do."

"How much?" She nailed him with a look. Mace averted his eyes, staring down at the digital camera in his hands before finally glancing in her direction.

"More than I should."

Jessie snorted. "Oh, come on, Mace! Let's get to the bottom of this, can we? I can't call you on your looks and your suggestive innuendos in the hotel or anywhere else, for fear of being overheard. Ordinarily, I wouldn't let that kind of word game go on without some kind of clarification on both parties' parts."

"This must be the new way relationships go?"

Shaking her head, Jessie said, "You loved a woman since you were a little boy in junior high school. Chances are you never dated since, right?"

"That's true."

"That's what I thought. Here's how it goes out there in the real world, Mace. Women don't play games anymore. We tell men what we want and don't want. It's up front. No more courtly rituals, I'm afraid."

"Pity," he murmured. Scratching his head, he held her glance. "Then you need me to be brutally honest about how I feel toward you? My intentions?"

"Exactly."

"I see…." He studied the camera in his hands again for several minutes before saying, "What if I don't know, Jessie?"

Her nostrils flared. "Oh, gimme a break, Mace! I see the look in your eyes. Tell me I'm wrong about it."

"What do you see?"

"That you want me. How much, or how far you want it to go, I really don't know. And honestly, I don't know if this is just the game you're playing because of our cover. I don't know *how* to take your advances."

"I didn't think I was advancing."

Jessie shook her head. "Well, you are whether you know it or not."

"I see…." he said again.

"Would it be helpful if I shared how I *really* feel about you?"

His heart pounded. Scared, he said, "Sure, I'd like to know." Gripping the camera a little tighter, he tried to prepare himself for bad news.

"I like you. A lot. At first I felt sorry for you, for your loss of Jillian. But I believe that we connected when we talked about your years of grief and the need for you to get on with your life. I'm interested in you and a possible future. And I need to know if you have a real interest in me or not."

Mace studied her profile. She was so capable, confident and strong. "I like you, too, Jessie. I'm in a wrestling match with myself, though. Our make-believe situation makes it real handy for me to look at you, absorb your beauty and smile, and hope. But I'm afraid, too. Afraid to really reach out again. I have this fear inside me, reasonable or not, that keeps telling me that if I get interested in a woman again, I'll lose her, too."

Chapter 8

Choking back unexpected tears, Jessie paid strict attention to flying the bird to their destination in Repulse Bay.

"Don't get me wrong, I like pretending this marriage is real. Like last night, when I went to bed with you." Mace's voice dropped and he said huskily, "You have no idea how sweet that was for me. I've missed lying next to a woman, knowing that her warm body, her breath, is a part of me. After you've been married for a long time and your partner is torn from you, the worst of it is a lonely, cold bed at night. There's no one to turn to and pull into your arms…no one to talk to, laugh with, play with…or just hold when the world sucks."

Wrestling with her own feelings, she finally managed to say, "I appreciate you telling me how things are. I guess if I was used to sleeping with someone every night and he was suddenly torn out of my life, I'd miss him terribly, too." She was sure she would.

Mace opened his hands in a helpless gesture. "I'm trying to be honest about this, Jessie. I don't have all the answers. And I don't want to mislead you, either."

Below them the dark green ocean sparkled, dappled with sunlight across its smooth surface. Tankers and container ships of all lengths and sizes plied the waters that comprised a huge port of entry for China.

"So, am I to assume all your attention is really about me being a replacement for Jillian?" Jessie had to ask the question. She didn't like the idea of being a stand-in for a dead wife, but she understood how it could happen, a realization that hurt nonetheless because she was genuinely drawn to Mace as a man. But if he was not seeing her, rather imposing Jillian on her, that wasn't good.

Giving a low whistle, Mace looked over at Jessie. Her profile was unreadable. It was the shape of her full lips, now thinned, that told him his answer had a lot riding on it. "You asked the right question and I'm not sure of the answer yet.

Do you fill a deep need to have a woman's warm body next to mine again? Yes. Am I simply reliving what I had with Jillian…? I'm not clear on it myself—yet." Mace gazed out the cockpit window. "I don't mean to confuse you. I'm just sorting all of this out myself right now, minute by minute. I'm sure this doesn't help answer your question, or does it?"

With a strained laugh, Wild Woman said, "Maybe I asked it the wrong way. Let me try again, because I want to be as clear as I can be. Every time you look at me, do you see Jillian instead?"

"No."

"Is there any time you see her and not me?"

"Yes, in bed last night. The memories…"

Wild Woman began banking the helo down over the busy city of Aberdeen, now beneath them. "So, you're reacting based on the past in some ways, and in others you're reacting based on the present, with me?"

"Well stated. Yes."

"So when we get to Marston's place and put on our cuddly husband-wife show, if I kiss you and you return it, I will wonder three things. Are you kissing me because of some undercover role? Are you kissing Jillian? Or are you kissing *me*?"

"If I kiss you, it would be because you're you. Not Jillian."

"Okay, that's a good enough answer."

"When you're kissing me, where are *you?* Is it only make-believe or real?"

Her mouth pulled into a grin. "Oh, no, dude, I'm kissing *you*. And I *want* to kiss you, okay? There's no confusion on my part about how I see you and me."

"Attraction 101," Mace murmured. Yeah, he could hardly *wait* to kiss Jessie, to taste her spirit, her fire, and absorb her passion for life into himself. In some ways Mace wondered if he was becoming an emotional vampire, needing to suck life from others in order to feel alive once more. That wasn't a pleasant thought and he didn't want to hurt Jessie in that way. It was obvious she was sincerely attracted to him, and that made him feel good about himself in a way he hadn't felt in a long time.

"You could say that, but even if I'm attracted to a guy, that doesn't mean I necessarily want to kiss him or go all the way. Like I said before, I'm slow to make it to bed with a man. Sex is great, but I was taught it was a final gift of love between a man and woman. And I've lived my life with that philosophy."

"I respect that and I'll certainly respect you for it," Mace said. "Being undercover as a married couple doesn't mean we have to have sex. I understand that."

"Good, because we have to step up our act starting tomorrow, and I need to be clear about us. What is genuine. What is not."

"I'll always tell you what is genuine, Jessie, if we're in a situation where I can say those words. Okay?"

Sunlight lanced brightly into the cockpit. Jessie turned up the air-conditioning to cool the heated interior. "Okay, you've got a deal."

She referred to the coordinates she'd entered from their flight plan. "What now? It looks like we're heading toward Stanley, on the southwestern tip of the island?"

Craning his neck, Mace looked at the terrain below. "Yes, that's Stanley coming up. Its claim to fame is the Stanley Market, the biggest weekend trade fest in the world. Anything you want to buy can be found. A lot of horse trading goes on. The Chinese like to haggle."

"I'm good at haggling. And horse trading comes natural to us Cheyenne. We're real horse people."

"I'll bet you are." He pointed to the community below, and the ship traffic coming and going in Repulse Bay. "This town is my favorite part of the island. It's not built up like the rest of it. It's pretty rural, and a lot of farmers make their homes in the area. Part of any weekend at the market is buying and selling vegetables, animals and fruit."

"Sounds like a lot of fun. I wish we had time to drive there and see it."

"We don't. At least not this trip. This jaunt is

strictly for show." Mace busied himself readying the camera. "Okay, let's make a turn and head back to Victoria Peak. Marston's villa sits on the northern slope, which looks toward Victoria Harbour and downtown Hong Kong. I'm going to take a number of photos, and once we get back to our hotel, I'll dump them on the computer and we'll analyze them. When we go to his place tomorrow at noon, we need to be aware of entrance and exit points in case something happens. We also need to know where we can hook up if we get separated. This is what we came for, so let's get started."

"Look at this," Jessie said as she leaned over Mace's shoulder and pointed to the large screen of the Mac G5 laptop. The image was Lihua, Marston's villa. "The place is pretty well obscured by that wall and by all those tall trees."

Mace studied this first of many photos along with Jessie. They had flown back to the hotel and tethered the helicopter on the roof. Choosing a quiet lounge on the fifth floor instead of their bugged suite, he'd set up his laptop so they could view the photos he'd taken of Marston's place. He could smell the faint fragrance of lilac as Jessie leaned close.

"This isn't uncommon among the wealthy," he told her, pointing to the pink, ten-foot-tall stucco wall that surrounded the complex. "The rich and famous around the world have either wrought-iron fences or high stone walls with security guards to make sure no one gets in to steal what they have."

Zooming in on the photo, Mace saw that there was concertina razor wire along the top of the wall, deftly camouflaged by the large, flowering trees. "Marston hasn't gone to any more lengths than the rest."

Jessie sat down next to Mace, their knees touching as the next photo appeared on the screen. "I wonder if there are any exits in that sloping backyard." The main house, made of steel, glass and stucco, looked like an architectural wonder. The compound included a series of round buildings attached to a larger one in the middle.

"Look at that!" Jessie said. "He's got a medicine wheel on his lawn."

Mace zoomed closer, focusing on a circle of white rocks, with five in different colors. "A medicine wheel?"

"Yeah, we use it in certain ceremonies. Powerful ceremonies. The wheel represents the universe, in a spiritual sense. It is an important part of our culture."

"Look over here." Mace pointed to the edge of the photo. "Teepees. Three of them. Looks like he's really putting a lot of thought into this Wild West barbecue of his."

Snorting, Jessica eyed the teepees. "Yeah, obviously."

"It doesn't sit well with you?"

"Hell no, it doesn't! He's 'playing Indian'! He's taking our culture, our way of life, and trotting it out as entertainment for people who won't appreciate the sacredness of any of it." She gripped her hands into fists. "I didn't know what to expect, but now I think I do. He's just showing off what he knows…and I'll bet he doesn't have a clue about the wheel."

"But doesn't it show how much he's immersed himself in Native American culture?" Mace saw the grim look on her face as she sat, hunched in the chair, glaring at the computer screen.

"Sure does."

"Maybe you can work that to your advantage."

"What do you mean?"

"You'll be dressed in your nation's clothing, with the medicine pouch at your side. Like Houston said, Marston will zero in on you because of that. And if that's so, Jessie, the medicine wheel is your opportunity to play him big-time. That's what this is all about—getting his attention, then manipulating him into letting us find out if he has that wolf's head crystal."

Giving Mace an admiring look, she reached over and squeezed his broad shoulder. "You're thinking on your feet. I was getting overemotional about this. Thanks. You're right. I need to keep this in perspective and remind myself why I'm here."

He liked the feel of her fingers on his shoulder. The small lounge was off the beaten path, so they were alone there. The space was quiet, intimate. Dangerous.

"Keep your eye on the ball, as naval aviators say," he told her with a brief smile as he posted a third photo. "You're the bait, Jessie. A beautiful lure. I don't think Marston is going to be able to ignore your presence when you walk into that party tomorrow. I know I wouldn't."

She playfully struck his shoulder. "Well, you're a little prejudiced, don't you think, dude?"

"Yeah, maybe a little." A lot, but he didn't want to say that. Right now, Mace was continuing to sort out his past from the present. Jillian would always be a part of him, and he never wanted to forget what they'd shared as a couple. But Jessie was right. He needed to put the past into perspective. And he needed to get on with his life. Judging from the twinkle in her eyes and from their candid conversations, she wanted to share her life with him to some degree. Mace wanted that, too. How much, he didn't know. There were no immediate answers, and where they were going tomorrow, life would become even more tentative. If Marston suspected they were spies, he had guards who, at a snap of his fingers, would readily kill them and dump their bodies into the South China Sea, where they'd never be found.

That thought made Mace's heart ache. Looking at Jessie as she intently studied the next photo on his computer, he was struck again by her womanly strength, a steely foundation beneath a soft exterior. Yes, she was the right person to go head-to-head with Marston. Mace knew he couldn't pull it off; he wasn't Native American, for starters. Already he found himself frustrated and worried that if Jessie got in trouble, he might not be at her side to help or to stop it. The mere thought served to compound his fears. Because for the first time since his loss of Jillian, he had found something to live for. Only, just like Jillian, Jessica Merrill could very well slip from his grasp.

The colorful, sparkling lights of Hong Kong glimmered in the distance. Milky radiance from the full moon illuminated wavelets across the dark waters of Victoria Harbour. From their huge bed in the penthouse, Jessie and Mace could witness the beautiful sight. She lay facing the panorama, having drawn back the curtains and sheer panels beneath to observe it. Mace lay nearby and she was acutely aware of his presence, the heat of his body. Between them was a sheet she'd draped over her hips. Mace lay on top of it, and Jessie sensed that the soft linen, although a flimsy barrier, served as a wall between them.

"It's a lovely city, isn't it?" she whispered. Knowing full well that the place could be bugged, she was once again in undercover mode, but didn't like having to think before she spoke. She twisted to look in Mace's direction. He lay propped up on several pillows, his chest bare, his lower body clothed in pale blue pajama bottoms. His hands were linked behind his head, his shadowed face pensive.

"What I'm looking at is even more beautiful."

Searching his darkened eyes, Jessica allowed the compliment to sink in. It touched her heart, which beat a little harder at his husky endearment, and it flowed like warm liquid down through the center of her body, nestling deep within her. She felt like a flower receiving the warmth of the sun after a long, cold winter. Well, hadn't she been in a winter of sorts for nearly four years now because of her black ops assignment? *No kidding!* And having a meaningful relationship with a man was something she'd been craving. Something ongoing, something that deepened over time. But that hadn't happened—until now.

She smiled tentatively at him. "What I'm looking at right now is a knockout, too. Hong Kong is nice, but, believe me, I'd rather look at you."

"Compliments will get you everywhere, luv...." Mace eased a hand from beneath his head and rolled onto his side to face her. He didn't want to push

Jessie. She'd said she was interested, and that was good enough for now. He didn't want to rush her. He'd learned a long time ago, with Jillian, that something good and lasting came with time and patience.

He reached out now and touched the blond bangs that grazed Jessie's dark brows. Sliding his fingers into the shockingly silky strands of hair, he murmured, "I like to see the lights of Hong Kong reflected in your eyes."

Absorbing his touch, Jessica closed her eyes. How she yearned to scoot closer and press her body against his. The temptation was so acute! Did he know how he was teasing her? Making her yearn to kiss him, to move her hands over the smooth muscles of his shoulders and chest? Entangle her fingers in that dark hair that made him look so damn male and dangerous? Jessica thought not. As she opened her eyes and met his burning gaze, she saw sincerity there. And hope. Hope for them? For a future together?

She whispered to Mace, "My people believe that you can see the soul of a person in their eyes. It's mirrored within them." Reaching out, she rested her arm against his waist. She could feel the heat of his flesh beneath hers. The itch to explore him was palpable. Oh, if only they didn't have to play this game of masquerade!

"Sometimes," she continued softly, holding his

gaze, "a person will let you into their deeper realms. That's when you can read a person's thoughts and feelings." She saw his lips part. The desire to touch his mouth, take it, consume it and become a part of him nearly drove her to do just that. The tension between them mounted. Jessie's whole body ached, starving for contact with his. Yet there was no way she was going to consummate a relationship here with Mace because she damn well wasn't going to have it witnessed or recorded. Not a chance in hell.

So she had to make do with looks, touches and whispered words.

"When I look into your exquisite eyes, I see the blue of the sky in them. You're like an eagle, luv, flying high above the rest of us. You see things in a way few people ever will. That's just one more thing I love about you...."

Love. For an instant, Jessie felt so connected to Mace that when he said that word, she believed it. But then she snapped out of her sweet trance and realized that he didn't really mean it. This was undercover patter, that was all.

Inwardly, she felt a pang of terrible disappointment. How she wished in this amazing moment with him that it had been *real*. That he'd used the word *love* with all of its power and meaning. Of course, he hadn't. Swallowing hard, she whispered, "We have a love that's stood the test of time, darling. And we can look into one another's eyes and see all we mean to each other."

To hell with it. Mace drowned in the liquid darkness of her wide, intelligent eyes. He moved closer. Something was driving him to touch her, to let her know on a nonverbal level that he meant everything he'd said. Yes, the word *love* had slipped out, unbidden, from his mouth. That hadn't been play-acting. And it had surprised him as much as her, judging from the shock he'd seen in her eyes when he'd whispered it to her. God, where did masquerade end and reality begin? Mace was unsure. As he moved even closer, he saw her gaze grow guarded and questioning.

"Come here…. All I want to do right now is hold you in my arms…." He held them out to her. Would she come to him? Would the sheet remain a barrier between them? Tonight, he wanted to hold Jessie— simply hold her. And he tried to show her that as he opened his arms for her to slide next to him. Seeing the hesitation in her eyes and the yearning, he wondered what she would do.

Jessie swallowed hard. Did she *want* to slide next to Mace? *Oh, yes!* Should she? What would happen?

Nothing *could* happen. Did he realize that? She hated the fact that she couldn't talk openly with him.

Trying to sort through her emotions, Jessie finally decided to hell with it. Mace had made it clear today where he stood with her. She rolled toward him, pressing herself against him. Where her body met his, even with the soft cotton sheet still between them, there was an incredible sense of warmth and protection. Laying her head against his naked shoulder, she settled an arm across his torso, hand draped against his hip. Heart pounding raggedly, Jessie had trouble keeping herself in check, much less worrying what Mace was going to do because she'd come to him.

"This...feels like ten million dollars," Mace whispered as he relaxed on the bed with her against him and moved a hand to the small of her back. He felt her laugh, which pressed her breasts momentarily against his chest.

"Twenty, fella."

Smiling, her hair tickling his nose and chin, Mace said, "Luv, you are priceless to me. No amount of money could buy what we have right now. I like it...." And he did.

Mace felt Jessie sigh and then surrender entirely, going limp and pliable against him. Oh, how he wanted to lean down and kiss her! But he didn't. This was enough. Plenty, in fact. He could feel his lower body hardening and, in a panic, he wondered if she would know. Of course she would. She was a mature woman. Grimacing, Mace tried to stop wanting to make love with her, but found it impossible. The peach-soft sensation of her skin against his, the delicate fragrance of lilac entering his flared nostrils nearly sent him spinning over the edge.

What stopped him was the fact that Jessie trusted him to do the right thing under the circumstances. She couldn't read his mind to know whether this was an undercover action on his part or a sincere attempt to hold her because it was what he wanted to do. No, this wasn't the right time to love her, although every cell in his body screamed that it was.

"Sweet dreams, luv."

"Oh, I'll have them, rest assured," Jessica said wryly, giving him a quick hug.

"It's going to be a busy day tomorrow," he told her quietly, returning her brief embrace. "And I wanted tonight to be special."

Closing her eyes, Jessie inhaled his male fragrance, which set every hormone in her body on alert. She smiled and nuzzled her face against his neck and jaw. "I understand, darling." This was exactly what she wanted—to be in Mace's arms. To be sharing herself with him.

As her heartbeat finally slowed, she turned her mind to their mission. Tomorrow, the dance with Robert Marston would begin. She knew he was clever. But just how clever? Was he a madman in disguise? Some twisted, evil person? Or just an eccentric who collected Native American artifacts because of an obsessive interest? Jessie wasn't sure. But she knew it would be a great mistake to underestimate the man.

Chapter 9

Robert Marston felt her arrive at his home with the power of a tsunami. It was a thrilling and completely unexpected sensation! He was very sensitive to other people's energy fields, which was why he routinely shielded himself from too much daily contact with people. Except for today, his yearly Wild West barbecue.

Sitting in his motorized wheelchair on the pink Italian marble patio, he motioned to Meng Du, a six-foot Chinese ex-army soldier who was his security guard, valet and helper.

"Go see who just arrived, Meng. Whoever it is, bring them straight to me."

"Of course, master."

Smoothing his carefully manicured silver goatee with trembling fingers, Robert turned and smiled at the crowds on the lawn below. Music—rustic hillbilly tunes—floated upward. The band of blue-grass players, had been flown in from Glen, Kentucky. There was plenty of laughter, the champagne was flowing faster than the servants could uncork and serve it, and everyone was eagerly mixing business with pleasure.

At least seventy-five people, millionaires, billionaires and celebrities, had taken him up on his invitation. And why wouldn't they? Power begat power, no doubt about it. Meng always bugged their hotel rooms and got photos of all his guests. But Robert had the flu and he hadn't seen all the reports on his guests.

Who had just arrived? Excitement thrummed through him. As he pushed his wire-rim bifocals back up his nose, he felt another wave of energy flow past him, much like a huge wave breaking on the shore. Who had that kind of power? No one he knew.

The whisper of the sliding glass doors opening captured his attention. He turned and his eyes widened. Before him stood a woman, obviously Native American, and a man, probably her husband. But what aroused Robert to a fever pitch was the fact that she was wearing traditional dress. Feeling like a slavering wolf approaching unsuspecting prey, he wheeled closer and saw that she was golden skinned. Her eyes were blue, which meant she wasn't entirely of Indian stock. Still, the deerskin vest she wore was undoubtedly authentic, delicately beaded in rainbow colors to form the design of snakes on either side, the cap sleeves fringed and the buttons definitely made from elk horn. Beneath the vest she wore a red calico ribbon shirt. And in her braided hair she had woven strands of red yarn, the color that symbolized East energy, at the base of which were attached white eagle fluff. From the tail feathers of a golden eagle, he'd bet. She wore a bright red sash around her waist.

Robert liked the fact that the woman wore pale gold buffalo-skin boots that came to just below her jeans-clad knees. The boots, too, had elk horn buttons and buffalo-skin laces.

Around her slender throat was a buffalo horn choker, from which dangled an eagle claw to show off, in a quiet kind of way, her energy. That of an eagle.

Robert remembered that a blue-and-silver helicopter had landed ten minutes ago. Meng had told him the arrivals were the new couple from Titan Industries. Well! This must be them! He gave them his most dazzling smile of welcome and moved his wheelchair even closer.

Wild Woman went on immediate guard. Marston looked frail sitting in his powered wheelchair, a gray Stetson cowboy hat on his head. He wore a black western shirt with white piping and pearl buttons. His terribly thin legs were encased in black trousers and he sported a pair of light tan ostrich-leather cowboy boots. Combined with his silver goatee and wire-rim glasses, he looked innocuous, but that was not what her instincts screamed. No, those watery gray-blue eyes ringed in black belonged to someone who was sinister enough to make her skin crawl.

As if sensing her chilled reaction to Marston, Mace extended his hand and protectively wrapped it around hers, squeezing reassuringly.

"Master Marston," Meng said in his deep, British-accented voice, "may I introduce Mr. and Mrs. Creighton Mason Webb. They are the owners of Titan Industries." Meng turned to them. "Please, meet Mr. Robert Marston."

Mace moved forward and took the man's thin, trembling hand. "Mr. Marston, it's a pleasure to meet you. This is my wife, Jessie. Luv, say hello to Mr. Marston."

Playing along, Jessie smiled. Marston's huge, close-set eyes honed in on her. Instantly, she felt her gut clench. Avoiding his sharpened appraisal, she extended her hand. "Mr. Marston, we're delighted to be invited. Thanks for having us."

She felt him squeeze her hand, hard. Surprised at his strength when he appeared to be so frail, she was taken off guard. As quickly as possible, Jessie disengaged from his handshake. She wanted to run screaming to the bathroom to scrub her hand. Keeping her smile in place with an effort, she returned to Mace's side.

"I am absolutely delighted to meet you. You, my dear...you're the real thing, aren't you?" He waved his hand at the crowd behind them. "They're dressed in costume, but you aren't, eh?"

"Yeah, I'm the real McCoy," Jessie said. "But I'm afraid I don't really fit in with all your fine feathered guests, Mr. Marston. I'm used to being at home, throwing a leg over my pony in Virginia or flying my husband's helicopter, ferrying him from one meeting to another."

Chuckling, their host said, "My dear woman, call me Robert. Only my enemies call me Mr. Marston."

His eyes lingered on the dark beaded leather bag tied on the left side of her belt. "I'll give you a million dollars for that little bag of yours."

Shock went through Wild Woman as he pointed with a wavering finger at her fake medicine bag. Marston knew exactly what it was. And that was why he wanted it. She had created the fake bag herself so he'd think it was real. Mike Houston had been right. She smiled and patted the bag gently. "I'm afraid not."

"Not for a million dollars?"

"Sorry, Robert. Some things just aren't for sale." Jessie lifted the bag in her fingers. "I assume you know what this is?"

"Of course. It's a medicine pouch."

"Oh, it's much more than that." Instantly, Jessie felt a shift of energy around him—a powerful one. Something kept bothering her about him. *What was it?* She wanted to back off, but knew she couldn't.

"Indeed?"

"This is my family's medicine bag. It's over four hundred years old and has been passed down from one generation to the next."

Eyeing it even more closely, he said, "I see.... I've heard of such things, but never seen one until now." He reached toward it. "May I?"

Jessie stepped back. "You mean you don't know the rules, Robert?" she teased. He didn't look very pleased at her adroit avoidance of his outstretched hand—a hand that suddenly seemed to resemble a claw to Jessie.

"What rules?"

"Red Road rules. I thought you had a fairly extensive understanding of Native American customs and knew about such things? At least, that's what I heard. There are strict dos and don'ts about touching something sacred that belongs to someone else." Wild Woman taunted him by patting the bag. "Unless someone offers their medicine bag to you, you do not reach out to touch it."

"Hmm. I wasn't aware of that." He had been, but wasn't going to let her know that. "I'll give you one point five million for it."

Turning to her husband, she said, "Darling, do we need another million and a half?"

"I don't think so, luv."

Marston cocked his head toward her husband. The man was dressed in casual business clothes— no tie, a dark blue blazer slung over one broad shoulder. "You have certainly been on my radar, Mr. Webb."

"Call me Mace," he murmured. "My friends use my middle name. And how am I on your radar, Robert?"

"I know little of Titan Industries. Of course, when Ji asked that you be put on the invitation list, Meng did a little research on you. Unfortunately, Ji called in sick, so he's not at the party today." Robert glanced favorably at Meng, who was dressed in a black uniform and starched white shirt, the weapon he always carried carefully concealed. Most of Marston's guests never realized that this six-foot-tall man from Beijing had been one of the fiercest combatants in the Chinese army, a throwback to the days of warriors. Meng never broadcast his power. Nor did Robert. He liked to throw people off balance by acting very warm, grandfatherly and kind toward them. He saved his venomous bite for when he didn't get his way.

Meng nodded. "Yes, master, Titan Industries is a low-key but highly successful corporation that has exclusive U.S. top-secret government contracts."

Mace smiled. "One doesn't have to be highly visible to make millions."

"True, so true," Marston murmured. "But you are a surprise. A delightful one for me." He turned his attention to Jessie. "My dear, you and your husband must partake of the feast below, fill your bellies and enjoy yourselves. Then you must come back up here. I have a very special showing just for you, Jessie. One that I think you'll appreciate."

The feast included barbecued deer, buffalo, pork and beef. After eating grilled buffalo meat, corn on the cob and red Texas beans that would burn anyone's gullet, Mace managed to maneuver Jessie to the tent where the bluegrass band was performing. There was a wood parquet floor, and he grabbed her hand and whisked her out among the couples who were two-stepping to the music.

Laughing, Jessie said, "Hey, you dance!"

With the music playing, Mace knew their conversation could not be picked up. He twirled her around, then slid his arm around her waist and brought her close. Not immune to the glances of a number of people, he knew they were being assessed. They were, supposedly, the new rich kids on the block. Not caring about that now, Mace pressed Jessie more firmly against him, his lips near her ear.

"Do you think he took the bait?"

Nodding, she said, "Yes. He's interested, Mace. I could see it and feel it."

"He wants to meet with you solo. You okay with that? You want me to go with you, anyway?"

Shaking her head, she whispered as she nuzzled his ear, "I'll go alone. I mean, he's an eighty-year-old man in a wheelchair. What's he going to do? Run me over with it? No, I can handle anything he throws at me."

"I have a bad feeling about this, Jessie. I don't like the way he looked at you."

Laughing, she kissed Mace's jaw and looked up into his eyes. "Jealous?"

"No. Worried."

Sobering a little as he spun her several times to the fast beat of the banjo and fiddle music, Jessie said, "There's something odd about him, Mace. I can't for the life of me put my finger on it, but I damn well feel it. It's bothering me. There's something…something my mother told me a long time ago and I can't recall…."

"Well, I saw the way he was salivating over that medicine bag. He wants it. He wants *you*."

Feeling Mace's arm tighten around her, his hand grip hers more firmly, Jessie smiled up at him. "That's what we wanted. Remember?"

"What if Meng goes with you?" he asked worriedly.

"So, he goes."

"That guy is dangerous. I'll lay odds he has a gun on him."

"Oh, he's a warrior," Jessie agreed, almost dizzied by the sudden twirls. She clung to Mace, laughing breathlessly as the music came to an abrupt halt. The couples on the dance floor separated and clapped and whooped loudly in appreciation of the four-piece band.

The next selection was soft and slow—just what Jessie hoped for. She turned and grabbed Mace, settling her arms around his shoulders and pressing herself fully against him. His eyes narrowed. She saw them burn with…what? Desire? Yes, she sensed his desire for her. Their hips melded and it felt good to feel his response to her. Looking beyond Mace to where Marston was perched on the patio, she saw that he had binoculars trained squarely on them.

"He's watching us like a hawk," she whispered to

Mace as she leaned up to press a kiss to his cheek. "He's got binoculars."

"Blatant, isn't he?"

Shrugging, she eased back. "It's his place. I guess if you're worth that much money, you can do just about anything you want, huh?"

"Not in my book," Mace growled, pulling her close and placing his jaw against her cheek. "You have the cell phone on you, right?"

They had agreed to keep their cell phones on vibrate. The press of a button would send a signal to the other that they were in trouble and needed help.

Jessie nodded. "Yep, primed and ready."

"Just be careful...."

Closing her eyes, Wild Woman pressed her face into his chest, inhaling his male fragrance. "You know what, Mace?"

"What?"

"You're my hero. It's been a long time since any guy thought I needed protection." Leaning away enough to see his darkening eyes, she added gently, "And I really can take care of myself, but it's nice to know there's a knight from King Arthur's round table just waiting to gallop in on his white steed should I require some assistance."

She broke free from Mace, gave him a quick, wifely peck on the cheek and turned toward Marston. It was time to dance with the devil.

As she strode confidently between groups of people, making her way to Marston, Jessie recognized actors and actresses from Hollywood, a few Hong Kong stars who had made it big in the U.S., several famous singers and a whole host of nameless faces she was sure were the rich but not famous. All of them were in costume to celebrate the Wild West theme, but she was the only real Indian. That made her feel strong and empowered in a way they would never understand.

When she reached the patio where Marston sat, binoculars in his lap, she gave him a teasing smile. "I'd ask you to do the two-step with me, but I'd probably get run over by that contraption you cruise around in."

"You have a sense of humor. I like that." Marston gave a high, girlish giggle and handed his binoculars to Meng before reaching out to grip Jessie's hand. "Come, my dear. I want to show you my etchings."

"And my husband?" Jessie inquired, pulling her hand from his.

"Meng is going to introduce him to one of my best friends, a software billionaire. I'm sure he'll be very interested in meeting him."

"Thank you for the thoughtful introduction."

Bowing his head, he said, "It is *my* pleasure, Jessie. Now, if you'll follow me, I want to show you my museum. I think you will be very impressed by what you see. Come, come...."

"Well, what do you think?"

Robert could see by the look on Jessie's face, the widening of her amazing blue eyes as she slowly turned in a circle, that she was overwhelmed by the beauty of his creation.

Soft Native American flute music floated around them as they stood in the first room of his museum, constructed entirely of his design. He'd had the architect build a circle of black granite because he knew that the wheel, the unending hoop of life, was important to Indians. He'd hired one of the foremost mosaic artists from Italy, Signora Raphella Benito, to create the floor beneath them, which depicted a medicine wheel. The background tile was black, the circle white. Within the circle was a perfect cross indicating the major directions, north, south, east and west, and an image of the animal that ruled each direction. Above them, four rectangular skylights allowed in natural light, and stationed around the room were red leather chairs.

"This is amazing," Jessie whispered, truly in awe. Her gaze moved quickly to the hundreds of artifacts that surrounded them, displayed behind glass. She did not see the crystal wolf totem. Why? Was he hiding it? More than likely. What wasn't hidden was the security guard stationed at a desk immediately inside the doors of this first room, Jessie noted.

"I thought you might like this place. I enjoy coming here and showing off my collection to the few who truly appreciate Native American artifacts. Have you looked beneath your boots to see what you're standing on?"

Gazing down, Wild Woman absorbed the details of the incredibly large medicine wheel. Taking a closer look at the animals, she was drawn immediately to the image symbolizing the north direction. Turning to Marston, she said, "You've patterned this after the Eastern Cherokee, haven't you?"

Surprised and pleased, he clapped his hands. "Why, yes! Yes, I have! Are you Eastern Cherokee?"

Shaking her head, Jessica looked again at the white bull buffalo that was the north energy symbol. "No, I'm half Northern Cheyenne and half Anglo." She raised her head to meet his excited gaze. "But I'd think a careful man like you, Robert, would already have done a pretty extensive background check on my husband and I. I think you know a lot more about me than you're willing to admit." She leaned down to run her fingertips across the white marble replica of the buffalo. It was an exquisite rendering of the mighty and majestic animal of the plains.

"Ahh, you are a clever wolf, aren't you?"

Straightening, Jessie faced him, her hands resting languidly on her hips. "Actually, a clever golden eagle."

"Yes, you are." He motioned to her choker and the claw suspended from it.

"Come, Jessie, look at what I've collected. I will value your knowledge regarding it...."

An icy feeling drenched her. The gleam in Marston's eyes told her he was a man obsessed—obsessed with her people's sacred objects. Wherever she looked, woven baskets, pottery and pieces of ancient fabric were displayed. But her intuition told her this was just window dressing.

She'd known all along that she had to force him to lead her into rooms two and three of his museum. Somewhere within them, she could sense the crystal wolf. And she would find it. One way or another.

Chapter 10

"Well," Robert said, pride in his tone, "what do you think of my world class Native American exhibit, Jessie?"

For forty minutes, Jessie had allowed Marston to show her all the woven baskets, grinding stones and pottery he'd collected for display in room one. Pretending interest, she'd said little about them and let him do all the talking.

"Very impressive."

He looked at her. "This room holds only some of my artifacts." Waving his hand, he said, "And these aren't really the important ones, but you may find them interesting, nonetheless."

"Oh?" She looked through the glass at baskets that had been woven by the Pima Indians of the Southwest. Some were very, very old. At least he'd made sure that the temperature and humidity were correct so that the artifacts wouldn't deteriorate as quickly. Of course, he'd told her as much, but on that point she didn't doubt him. Further, he'd had special lights installed that would not leach the color out of the textiles on display. Still, Jessie didn't like the idea of so many artifacts being in this man's hands. There was something so slimy about him that she could barely tolerate remaining in the huge rotunda with him. Something her mother had told her when she was very young flared anew, but remained just out of reach in the recesses of her early memory. Whatever it was, Jessie knew it was vital. And she knew Marston had just given her an opening.

"Are there more rooms to your museum?" she asked, gesturing toward a red door at the rear of the rotunda. Jessie glanced into his watery eyes and feigned a smile. There was something dangerous about looking into his eyes, and she felt a frisson of fear, like cold ice in the pit of her stomach, every time she connected with his gaze.

"I can tell you're rather bored with all this peripheral Native American paraphernalia," he said with a chuckle. Powering his wheelchair, he headed for the red door. "Come with me. I think this next room will better pique your interest. But we'll see...."

The door opened automatically after Marston wheeled up to a device that seemed to scan his eye. As Jessie followed him inside, her heart picking up in beat, she saw that the second room was round like the first. Also like the first room, the floor held a mosaic of a medicine wheel, only this one she recognized as the Sioux design for the four directions.

Marston stopped in the center of the room, the skylights above bathing him in natural light. "Have a look. See what I've collected. See if you recognize any of it."

She could hear the gloating in his voice. The pride. Hands behind her back, she slowly walked around the room's circumference, viewing the objects behind the thick glass. In this room were hand-beaded moccasins, beaded quivers that had once held arrows, knives ranging from the Plains 1800s to very old ones carved of pure obsidian. Jessie knew the obsidian knives were not North American; Central or South American would be her guess. She saw saddlebags, rifles and rifle sheaths with beading and fringe, but no wolf's head crystal.

"I recognize a couple of the moccasins as Northern Cheyenne," she told him as she continued her slow tour of the room. "There's a quirt with a beaded handle that looks Cheyenne to me, too."

"Correct," Robert said in a pleased tone. "I really don't have too much of North or South Cheyenne in this exhibit."

Jessie turned to Marston when she was done with her inspection. "I can tell you've spent a long time collecting these things."

"My whole life," he answered.

"What got you interested in Native American things, Robert?" It was better to know the enemy, Jessie felt.

"Ahh, an insightful question," he murmured.

"I'm always interested in what motivates people," she said, smiling briefly. Jessie watched as he stroked his goatee for a good minute before answering, obviously deciding what to tell her. Fine; she could be patient.

"Do you know anything about me?"

Shrugging, Jessie said, "Not really. Frankly, I have a life of my own and don't often stick my nose into other corporations or concerns."

"You don't have to. I'm sure your husband does."

"Of course. It's his business, not mine. But back to you. What got you into collecting native artifacts?"

"Ah, that…yes. Well, I was born in Toronto, and as a child, I had an absolute fascination with Native North Americans. My parents would take me on hunting and fishing trips to Banff, near Calgary in

Alberta, Canada. My father's guides were always Indian. I used to sit with them and listen to their
stories." He sighed. "I love Native American stories. They are like Aesop's Fables. There is always
something instructive about them. Of course, telling
their stories was how the people passed on the
knowledge of good behavior from bad and that sort
of thing."

"It's called walking the Red Road."

"Exactly." Robert gazed at her. She avoided meeting his eyes.

"So, I grew up with this insatiable hunger. One
of our guides, an old man from the Blood tribe, once
gave me a little nondescript gray rock. It had a hole
in it—a natural one. I think he took pity upon me—
a little eight-year-old, snot-nosed kid left on shore
while Father went out to fish for lake trout. The old
guide said the stone had power and that if I carried
it with me, I would find it to be of benefit. Well, I
was thrilled, to say the least. I tried to get that old
Blood to tell me about the stone, but he just shook
his head and told me to hold it and find out for myself."

"Right," Jessie murmured. "Our way of teaching
isn't to give you answers. We give you something
that will help you find them on your own."

"I discovered that the hard way," Robert said in-
dulgently, stroking his beard again. "Oh, I cried,

pouted, sulked and had temper tantrums trying to get that old man to tell me. He just looked at me with no expression on his face and said nothing. I felt like I was talking to a stone."

Even at age eight, Marston had been developing skills to manipulate people to get what he wanted. That was frightening to her. "So? Did you do as he said?"

"Finally, yes. I went over to a log on the shore and sat down with it. I held it, but nothing happened. I was furious."

"How much time did you wait, though?"

He clapped his hands again. "Precisely, Jessie. You know a child of eight has no patience at all. I probably sat there all of three minutes, squirming and waiting."

Grinning, Jessie said, "The Red Road is about patience. And waiting. And trying to put yourself into harmony so you can hear the Great Spirit's voice."

"Again, you're correct. At eight, however, I did not know any of that."

"What did you do with the stone?"

With a trembling hand, he pulled out a leather thong from inside his shirt. At the end of it was a small deerskin pouch. "It's here...."

Amazed, Jessie said, "So, you found out what it was all about?"

"What do you know about stones that have a natural hole through them?"

She heard the slyness in his voice. "I know what it means, if that's what you're asking."

"Tell me."

Shaking her head, Jessie said, "I can't do that."

"Why not?"

"Because it's sacred information."

"Ah, yes, I've heard that before from Native American medicine people." He cocked his head as he continued to look at her. "Your mother's a medicine woman. Practicing to this day, as I understand it?"

It bothered Jessie that he knew about her mother. Swallowing her fear, she said, "Yes, she's an elder on the Northern Cheyenne res of Lame Deer."

"So she steeped you in medicine way knowledge."

"Of course."

"And yet you aren't a medicine woman."

"No, I chose another way to walk the good Red Road." If he knew that she was an Apache combat helicopter pilot, he'd probably fall out of his wheelchair. Inwardly, Jessie gloated over that secret knowledge. Marston didn't know everything, fortunately.

"I think," he said, raising his white brows, "that you took after your mother's male ancestors."

"Oh?" Her heart beat a little harder in her chest. She felt his energy reaching out like invisible fingers, seeking to trap her and hold her in place.

"I know from your mother's lineage that her great-grandfather and the males before him were Dog Soldiers, the elite of Cheyenne society. The last line of defense for the tribe. In fact, I know that each Dog Soldier wore a sash that trailed the ground. Each one carried a sacred arrow in his quiver. When he met the enemy, he would place the sash on the ground and jam the arrow down into it. And it was there that he made his stand, no matter whether he lived or died. He defended that sash. He stood and fought."

Jessie nodded. "Yes, and there was a sacred song that only a Dog Soldier could sing. A song he sang as he rode into battle."

"A death song?"

"I can't say."

"You could."

"But I won't. It's a secret known only to the Dog Soldier Society."

Marston pointed to the red sash she wore around her waist. "That is a Dog Soldier sash."

"Very good, Robert," Jessie said.

"Did you think for a moment I wouldn't know what you were wearing?"

Shrugging carelessly, Jessie moved away to peer into one of the glass cases. "I didn't really think about it, to tell you the truth." *Liar.* But he didn't need to know that.

"And I know that medicine pouch you wear on your sash is very special, too. There's a lot of power to it."

Jessie looked over her shoulder at him. She could see Marston literally salivating like a rabid dog over what she wore. The man was obsessive-compulsive about Indian things. *Why?* The pouch he was fixated on had nothing of value in it. Beneath her clothing, however, in the small deerskin pouch hanging between her breasts was her real medicine bag.

"So, you chose to walk the path of the Dog Soldier instead of that of a medicine woman. What intrigues me is that they'd allow a *woman* into the ranks of this all-male society."

Laughing, Jessie turned to him, hands on her hips, feet spread apart like a boxer prepared to spar with an opponent in the ring. "Well, now, Robert, although you seem to know quite a bit about Cheyenne Dog Soldiers, you obviously didn't do enough digging around to find out that there were women in the society in years past—and today."

Stroking his goatee, he looked at her as if weighing her teasing words. "I know a great many people of the First Nations."

Shrugging, Jessie said, "So what?"

"So, I pay good money for good information."

"Oh, Robert, what we have isn't for sale at any

price! Sacred means secret. We don't give away sacred artifacts or the information about them. They belong to the tribe and nation."

Somehow, Jessie had to bait Marston into showing her the third room of the museum. Her gut told her that what she sought was in there. The first room had been innocuous, holding simple, everyday things that Native Americans used to survive. The second room displayed hunting and fighting tools. She saw nothing to suggest ceremonial items, which had to be in the last room. There was another red door here, and Jessie hungered to get into the room beyond. Her intuition told her the wolf's head crystal was in there.

"Yes," Marston murmured, "you're correct. But your reservations are poor, and money talks, you know."

"Maybe."

"No maybe about it, my dear. Tell me something?"

She walked closer to him, hands on her hips. "If I can. What?"

"Every medicine person carries a pipe."

"Where is this going?" Jessie asked.

"I know for a fact that Dog Soldiers were pipe carriers, too. So, are you a pipe carrier for your nation, my dear?"

"Yes, I'm a pipe carrier. A personal one, not a ceremonial one."

"Ah, yes…I know a great deal about pipes. Being chosen to carry one is a great honor, as I understand it."

Jessie turned and began walking the circumference of the room again. "A pipe carrier is a role model, Robert," she said, her voice echoing oddly in the chamber. "He or she must have integrity, be a good-hearted person and strive hard to always walk the Red Road." She wasn't telling him anything that was secret, but she also knew this information was not known to the general public. Hoping to bait him, she halted at the red door. "What's in here?"

"Are you drawn to it, my dear?" Robert said, chuckling. "Do you feel power throbbing out of it like ripples after a stone is thrown into water?"

"Yes."

"That's my secret room. I rarely show anyone what is in there."

Placing her hand on the door, she said, "I can feel what's in there, Robert."

"Really?"

"Yes."

Sizing her up, he whispered, "If you can tell me what's in there, I will show it to you. Let's just see how clairvoyant you are as a pipe carrier."

Though her heartbeat picked up a little, she laughed. "Pipe carriers aren't necessarily psychic, Robert. Is that what someone told you?" *Is that information you bought from some medicine person who want-ed money more than holding sacred the secrets of their nation?* How badly Wild Woman wanted to say that, but she bit the angry words back.

"Oh, come now! Of course you are! That pipe is *alive!* It is not some inanimate object. I know for a fact that there is a very powerful spirit in a pipe. And there is teaching that goes on between the carrier and the pipe itself."

Anger sparked within her. How much more did he know? Pipe knowledge was one of her people's oldest and deepest-held secrets. It simply wasn't shared with anyone who wasn't a pipe carrier. And yet this obsessed old man knew. She found that disgusting. Keeping her expression carefully neutral, Jessie said, "I can't confirm or deny it, Robert. We do have our secrets and our traditions."

"Tell me what's in that other room, Jessie, and I'll show it to you."

Knowing that she had hooked him, that he was more than ready to reveal the last of his hand to her, with a flourish she placed her palm against the door and closed her eyes.

"I haven't done this in a while," she confided. "But I'll give it my best shot."

Pretending to try to perceive what was inside, Wild Woman took a huge risk. "You know what I see, Robert?"

"Tell me...."

"I *feel* a quartz crystal.... Now, this isn't just any crystal—it's an animal...and the impression I'm getting is that it's a wolf?" She lifted her hand from the door, turned and pinned Marston with her gaze. "Well? Am I right?"

"Amazing! You are simply amazing! Yes, yes! That is correct!"

His voice had gone high and shrill, almost falsetto, with excitement. Jessie stepped aside as he zoomed up to the red door and pushed the button that would allow them inside.

Chapter 11

Wild Woman's breath hitched momentarily as she walked behind Marston into the third and smallest circular room. Her gaze quickly swept the area. She noted a narrow door off to the right between two display cases.

Her heart pounded once, hard. The crystal wolf's head!

As foretold by her dream, the totem slowly rotated on a green velvet cushion, allowing her to see it from every angle. It was awesome! No wonder Marston had stolen it! Jessie had to gulp several times to contain her reaction to the mighty ceremonial totem.

In this room, as she'd suspected, Marston indeed displayed powerful medicine objects used in sacred ceremonies. As she looked around her, her heart broke in anguish, then ballooned with anger. She saw at least fifty pipes, some very, very old. There were some made of clay and others made of brick red pipestone that could have only come from the one-of-a-kind quarry in Minnesota that nearly all nations went to. She saw other totems, as well. Some were rocks with holes in the center of them. Compressing her lips, Wild Woman swallowed hard against the righteous rage that was soaring up through her. Marston had probably stolen all of these pipes. Sometimes a pipe was given to a friend or family member, but it was *never* sold. And it was rare that a white man, no matter what country he was from, would ever receive a pipe from an Indian. It was a travesty of the worst kind, as far as she was concerned.

"You deserve to be rewarded, Jessie. Come, look at what your powers perceived." He pointed to the crystal object behind the thick glass.

Jessie stood beside Marston, hands behind her back as she gazed down at the wolf's head. She could feel the old man looking from her to the totem like an excited child.

"Well? What do you think?"

She turned to Marston. His eyes were alight with

enthusiasm, his hands clasped in his narrow lap in expectation. "It's quartz crystal. I recognize it as one of the clan totems of the Eastern Cherokee people."

"Why, yes! You are amazing! You're Cheyenne and yet you know so much about another nation's sacred objects."

"I have many friends from many nations, Robert. All nations get together at powwows. It's a pretty limited society, when you look at it that way. There aren't a whole lot of Indians left."

"Lucky for me," he crowed, smiling widely. Pushing his glasses back up on his nose, he gestured around the room. "I call this my power room."

"Oh?" Jessie wanted to cry as she looked at her people's sacred pipes displayed artfully and carefully for the enjoyment of one opportunistic man. If her mother saw this, she'd explode into a rage, breaking the glass cases and taking all the pipes out of here. That was what Jessie would like to do, but it was impossible. Recovering the wolf's head totem was her sole mission.

"Well," Robert said, stroking his beard with trembling fingers, "this is a closely kept secret, but I was diagnosed with Parkinson's disease thirty years ago, when I was fifty. I hated it! I didn't want to turn into some hobbling, crawling, sniveling old man. I knew from collecting totems and artifacts from around the world and from many indigenous cultures that each piece had inherent power." He guided his wheelchair to one Native American pipe display. "If you're a pipe carrier, you know that each pipe has power."

"That's right, it does," Wild Woman murmured, following him to a green velvet wall display where at least twenty pipes were mounted.

"I have yet to crack the code beyond that," he told her, regret in his tone. Wagging his finger at the collection, he said, "But despite what I didn't know about a pipe, I knew they possessed the most power of any ceremonial tool the Native American culture had. Of course, that's a generalization. I have a few other artifacts in here that are equal to or even more powerful than the pipes in my collection."

"The older the medicine object, the more powerful it is," Jessie agreed. "And pipes aren't the only thing we use to create contact with the Great Spirit."

"How true, how true." Excitedly, he wheeled his chair to a display case and poked his finger against the glass. "You see that old clay pipe in the back? The one with the red-and-green painted stem? With diamond shapes carved into the wood?"

Peering into the case, Jessie said, "Yes, I see it."

"Any guess as to what nation it belonged to?"

"Hmm…let me think. Well, most Plains nations got their pipe material from the pipestone quarry in Minnesota, so it can't be one of them," she murmured. That, of course, was something Robert would already know. Realizing he was rabid for *new* information, she purposely led him on. "And the Calf Bone Pipe of the Lakota, Dakota and Santee nations was created from the bone of a buffalo's lower front leg, so that's not it." She pretended to reexamine the pipe and consider her answer. Feeling Marston's barely held excitement, she let him sit there and sweat it out. Finally, she said, "This one is made from clay, huh? The Southwestern cultures didn't have access to the pipestone quarry far to the north of them. This pipe was fashioned in Arizona, I would guess. And I believe it's either Yavapai or Apache. I don't know which." She turned and looked down at him. The look of absolute glee on his face made his pale skin seem almost rosy for a moment.

"It is Yavapai. You are simply amazing! I don't know what stroke of good luck brought you to me, but I'm overwhelmed. And there isn't much that gets me this excited at eighty years old."

Jessie smiled at him and said, "I'm glad I could be of a little assistance to you, Robert. Tell me more about your power room." She wanted to understand his obsession with these artifacts. A man of power collecting power? Sure, that was entirely possible, but Jessie felt there was more to it.

Robert pulled a white silk handkerchief from his back pocket and mopped his damp brow. Looking

at his trembling hands, he told her, "When I was diagnosed with this damnable disease, I spent millions on every imaginable treatment to get rid of it.
None of them worked, of course. Right now, I have
a gene tech company doing research on the condition. When they finally find the DNA sequence to
heal it, I will be given shots that will destroy this
cursed illness. They estimate it will be five years yet
for a cure. A long time to wait…"

"Yes, but thirty years ago, genetic technology
wasn't even around."

"No, it wasn't. So you're right, I've already faced
many more years of scrambling to try to stop this disease. I had a particularly virulent form of it, so I had
no time to waste. I went to hands-on healers from
Russia. I went to Filipino psychic surgeons. I went
to the best neurologists money could buy and all
they could do was give me drugs that took away my
quality of life." He looked fondly at the display of
pipes. "And all the time, the answer I needed was
right in front of me."

"What do you mean?" Jessie felt a sense of dread
as she watched Marston gaze at the pipes.

"I had been collecting Native American ceremonial items for decades. I knew from what little I
could get out of certain medicine men that every object was imbued with power. A *lot* of power." He
flexed his right hand, opening, then closing it into a

fist. "When I was still a young man, I was down in Brazil. One old, greedy bastard of a medicine man offered to show me how to pull energy off anything I wanted it from. I paid him handsomely and through an interpreter he taught me how to do it." Grinning evilly, Robert whispered, "And it works."

Alarm flooded Jessie. "He taught you to—" she wanted to use the word *steal* but didn't "—take power from something?"

"Oh, not just some things, certain things, my dear." Gesturing to the pipes, he said, "As soon as I got Parkinson's, I decided to use the technique and see if I could pull power off one of these pipes to help combat my symptoms." Cackling, he looked up at her, pride in his tone as he declared, "It worked!"

Jessie struggled to keep her face neutral. *Play dumb,* she told herself, *play dumb. Don't let him know that you know how the technique works.*

"What worked, Robert?"

"Well, I was able to suck the energy out of a pipe. And when that happened, a tingling would begin in my hands. Then I'd feel this vibrating power speeding up and down my spine, then into my arms and legs. It's an incredible event, let me tell you!" He smiled delightedly. "With just one pipe, I could stop the progression of my disease for about three to six months, depending, of course, on how much power the pipe had within it. I came to realize that whoever had the pipe had a lot to do with the amount of power it held. Using each pipe that I have here, I began to see a lessening of my symptoms. Over the years, my aggressive form of Parkinson's has been slowed to a record crawl. My doctors, of course, shake their heads and don't understand why I wasn't six feet under at age sixty, because that's how long they gave me to live."

Robert gestured to the artifacts surrounding them. "These objects that you see in these cases all gave their energy to keep me alive so that I could be here to take advantage of the DNA genetics that will stop this damnable disease once and for all."

Sickened, Jessie tried to keep the rage out of her tone. "And this wolf's head totem? Have you taken the energy from it yet?"

Frowning, Marston said, "No...I was hoping to use two others first, but those plans have fallen through."

"I see." Her mind whirled with anger and anguish. Those pipes were as alive as any human being. Robert Marston was a sorcerer. For it was sorcery, a disempowering of another individual, thing or in this case, a sacred implement of the Native Americans, which he had stolen without their permission. He was an energy thief. As she stood beside Marston in his power room, Jessie finally understood what she had felt around him from the beginning. He was a psychic vampire of the worst kind, trained in the stealing of other people's energy. In this case, he had honed in on sacred objects, but she wouldn't be surprised if he knowingly leached energy from anyone around him who would allow him to do so. He was a sorcerer, plain and simple. No wonder she'd gotten a warning chill down her spine.

Swallowing against a dry throat, Jessie said, "I don't think you'd find much energy with that clan totem, anyway, Robert," she said in a bored tone.

"Oh?" He looked up at her. "You know something that's more powerful?"

Jessie began to slowly walk around the room, her mind churning with a spontaneous idea. "Oh, Robert, these totems are, if you'll pardon my bad pun, low on the totem pole of sacred and powerful objects that the Eastern Cherokee people have."

"Really?" He turned his wheelchair around to follow her. "Tell me more."

Jessie halted at the small door between the two displays to quickly examine it. It had a brass doorknob and beside it on the doorjamb a square console with nine number keys. The outer door had opened by iris recognition. Robert's iris. This one was different, yet in some weird way familiar to her. She needed to know more about it, but right now, she had to scramble to set him up with her plan.

"I have a good friend on that res. Her name is

Grandmother Ivy." Peering over at Robert, Jessie said, "Perhaps you've heard of her?"

"Indeed I have. She is the chief elder of the medicine women of that nation. Very old. Very wise."

"And *very* powerful, Robert. Frankly—" Jessie gestured toward the totem "—I think you're barking up the wrong tree with this wolf's head crystal. From what I understand, there are more powerful objects that would be of interest to you...."

Would he take the bait? She saw his pale blue eyes sharpen, his lips part in expectation. He rolled his wheelchair to where she stood.

"What? What objects have more power?" He jabbed his finger at the pipe display. "More power than a pipe?"

Laughing, Jessie said, "Oh, Robert! You could combine everything you have in this room and it would be a pittance compared to them!" She saw his face flush, his eyes dance with excitement.

"Tell me! You *must* tell me, Jessie!"

"Why should I?"

"Because you don't want to see me rot away with this damn disease, that's why."

"What's in it for me?"

He sat back and gave her a feral look. "Ah, I see...."

"My husband and I are looking for new worlds to conquer with his software innovations. We need contacts. Now, if you could tell your friends about us, get Mace's salespeople into the offices of corporations around the world, I would consider that a fair trade. Wouldn't you?"

Jessie knew if she didn't play hardball, Marston would suspect her motives. If she just gave him information without wanting something of equal value in return, he might not believe her. Or might think he was being set up. Holding her breath, Jessie watched as he stroked his goatee, his white brows knitting.

"My dear, you have a deal." He reached out and shook her hand. "I'll tell Meng to put my global team to work on getting you a red carpet into every corporation you've ever desired to do business with." He wagged his finger at her. "However, I will *not* initiate that course of action until you first tell me what is so powerful, and I have it in my possession. And it must work. Then and only then will I give you the information and support you require. Deal?"

He was a shrewd bastard, but then, Jessie knew he'd made his billions by being a brutal corporate strategist and tactician. Grinning widely, she said, "Deal, Robert."

"Excellent! Now, tell me, what do the Eastern Cherokee have that is so powerful."

"You might already be aware of it, Robert. I'm sure you'll tell me. They have what is known as the Ark of Crystals."

His brows flew upward. "Why, yes! Yes, they do. I've heard about them. Seven quartz crystal points that symbolize the seven clans? I thought—er, understood—that the clan totems, also made of crystal, were in that ark, as well."

"That's true."

"You've *seen* the ark?"

"Many times." What a lie! She had to rely on Kai Alseoun's information now, and Jessie prayed it was accurate.

"Tell me what you saw," he demanded, his voice turning brusque.

Now the steel-coated bastard came out. *Fine.* Jessie continued her walk around the room. "The ark is kept by a medicine man from the Yam Clan. That's the clan charged with care and protection of the ark. In the ark are seven totems. The one you have, the wolf's head, symbolizes the Wolf Clan. What you may not realize is that there is a false floor in the bottom of the ark. That is where seven crystals wrapped in seven different colors of cloth are kept. They hold the *real* power, Robert. Each crystal is roughly ten inches long and about three inches wide, and each comes to a single point. When they are brought out, which is only four times a year, to honor the turning of the seasons, the power they bestow upon those who take part in the ceremony is incredible." Turning on her heel, she pinned Marston with a dark look.

"There is *nothing* that compares to the power of those crystals. Everything else is secondary, like a wire carrying electricity. The crystals are the big generator, the Hoover Dam." She hoped he would take the bait.

"And how does Grandmother Ivy factor…"

"She is friends with the medicine man caretaker from the Yam Clan. Because she's the head elder, she is the only one able to work with the crystals during these four yearly ceremonies."

"I see…. And this old woman can get her hands on the crystals for me?"

Jessie ambled back to where Marston sat, his face wrinkled in thought. Planning how to get his hands on the crystals, she was sure. "That's right."

"Then you can get her to give them to you?"

Laughing, Jessie shook her head. "Oh, no, Robert! She's the only one who can handle them. I can't. I'm not a medicine person, nor am I trained to deal with their energy."

Salivating at the prospect, he whispered excitedly, "Well, tell me how I can get them!"

"I need to make some phone calls," Jessie demurred. "Grandmother Ivy doesn't have a phone, but I know someone near her who does. I can contact her that way."

"How much will she want for them?"

"How much are you willing to pay?" Jessie

thought it amazing how Marston believed everything was for sale. There was no way the Eastern Cherokee nation would ever sell any of its treasured sacred objects, particularly the crystals in the ark. The elders would sacrifice their lives to keep such a travesty from occurring.

Throwing up his hands, Marston said, "What do you think she'll ask?"

"She'd probably be satisfied with ten million apiece." Jessie knew the crystals were priceless, but had to throw out some number to play Marston's game.

"That's seventy million."

"Yes. Worth every penny, in my opinion. What's your life worth to you?" By now, Jessie knew he relied on her opinion. It was a heady moment. This was power of a different sort, and it felt good to be utilizing it against an energy thief like Marston.

"Very well!"

"You'll have to wire the money to a Swiss bank account, Robert. I'll provide the number. And I will verify that the money's there before you get the crystals. If the deal doesn't go through, for whatever reason, you'll get all your money back."

"Done! I'll call Meng right now to make it happen!"

"You're going to have to personally collect the crystals from Grandmother Ivy, Robert. Like I said, she won't hand them over to me; only to you, I'm sure. You're the buyer. I can be there as the middle person brokering this deal, but you'll have to fly to Asheville, North Carolina, to get the crystals." She saw him instantly pale, his eyes widening with shock.

"No! I can't do that! That's impossible!"

Pretending ignorance, Jessie asked, "Why? I don't understand. Is your health so bad you can't fly in your corporate jet?" Marston had a jumbo jet at his disposal, and Jessie knew he had every comfort on board. No, what terrorized him was the thought of entering the U.S. If he did, law enforcement authorities could place him under arrest for theft of archeological objects, for starters. She saw beads of sweat popping out on his wrinkled brow as he sat there, fidgeting nervously. She could feel him weighing the thought of being caught versus the thought of getting his hands on those powerful crystals.

"I don't know…. I must think…." He mopped his brow. "I'm not welcome in the United States anymore, my dear."

"I'm sorry, I didn't know." But she did know she was doing a high-wire act, trying to appear less bothered by his statement than his being denied access to a possible cure. "Why not enter through Canada under an assumed name? They won't suspect you that way, will they?" Of course, she'd alert Mike

Houston and he'd get the proper authorities in line to follow every step of Marston's entrance into the U.S.A.

"Yes…yes, something could be arranged. But this is such a risk…." He gave her a dark, assessing look. "And it could be a trap."

"I don't know why you would say this is a trap, Robert." She decided to confront him on the accusation. Her heart raced with trepidation.

"A trap to get me within U.S. boundaries." He continued to squint up at her, his mouth thinning with displeasure.

"I don't know what you're talking about." She opened her hands and gave him what she hoped was an innocent look. "Listen, if you don't trust me, please check our backgrounds. I know we do deep security checks on people we employ. I've got to think you have a whole department that does nothing but this kind of research on individuals or corporations you're planning to do business with. So let's not do anything until you feel you can trust me."

Marston mopped his brow again, obviously torn between wanting to trust her and fearing to. The moments dragged by, the silence deepening between them.

"All right, all right. Let me think about this," he said in an irritated tone. "I will check you out. Thoroughly. No Swiss bank account until I'm positive this is not a trap!" He looked at his watch. "We've been gone an hour, my dear. I think I must return to my guests. I can't completely ignore them."

Relieved, Jessie said, "I understand. And I really should get back to my husband." She smiled softly. "Before we leave, can you tell me where this little door leads? I noticed that the other doors were painted red, but this one isn't."

Turning his wheelchair toward the narrow door between the displays, he said, "Oh...that. Well, that's an access door. Through there my conservator and other workmen can get behind all three rooms of the museum. Someone has to care for the artifacts and the premises." He gave her another dark look. "Just remember, I have people on duty twenty-four hours a day. In fact, almost hourly someone checks the humidity and temperature in each display case. And my guards shoot first and ask questions later if anyone tries to break in with the thought of stealing my precious possessions."

"I'm fascinated with all the safety precautions you've taken. I never realized—"

He waved his hand. "My dear, there are people in the world who would steal everything I've acquired. There's a huge black market for it. But you obviously don't realize that," he said impatiently, then seemed to remember his manners and smiled. "If you want, take a walk around there. You'll see that a concrete sidewalk circles the back side of every rotunda. Follow it toward the entrance to the museum and I'll meet you there."

"Great!" Jessie went to the door. "Do you need a code to open this door?" Her heart beat hard. Robert Marston was so caught up in his excitement to get the seven crystals from the ark that she hoped he wouldn't be as wary as he might be under other circumstances.

"Oh...yes...that."

He wheeled to the panel and punched a series of keys. Jessie glanced furtively at the red numbers on the console, burning them into her memory before quickly looking away: 2242.... The door clicked open. "Thanks," Jessie said as she slipped into the dark area. "I'll see you out front, Robert!"

Closing the door, Jessie allowed her eyes to adjust. Sure enough, there was a wide concrete catwalk bordered by a pipe railing. The walkway was lit, but otherwise the space was dark. Moving quickly, Jessie hurried around the rotunda to the display case that held the crystal wolf's head.

The case was not locked! Just a simple sliding door offered the only obstruction. Such was Marston's belief in his impenetrable security system. Moving to the sliding glass window of the display case, Jessie studied the totem. Less than two feet away was the object of their mission. Her hands itched to grab the blazing crystal wolf's head, but now was not the time. Not yet…

Hurrying toward the entrance, Wild Woman finally saw the exit door and pushed it open. She couldn't wait to tell Mace her plan to nail Marston and get back the wolf's head.

Chapter 12

"Tell me everything," Mace said once they were airborne. "You looked a little flushed when you came back from the museum, and I know you couldn't say much at the party."

After she'd rejoined him, they continued the social chitchat for a while, and around dusk said their goodbyes to their host. Robert had told Jessie to stay in close touch about their "little project."

Jessie glanced at the fuel gauge and said, "If it's okay with you, I'm going to fly around Hong Kong for a while before we go back to the hotel. I'm so damn nervous, I need to unwind and start breathing again."

"I understand. So, what went down?" His curiosity was burning. To him, Jessie looked cool, calm and collected, but there was more color in her cheeks than when she'd come back from the museum with Marston.

Wild Woman told him everything as she guided the helicopter over the South China Sea. The sun had just set, leaving in its wake a rosy-pink ribbon of color across the horizon as the waves darkened beneath them.

Scratching his head, he murmured, "That was some fast thinking on your part. It's amazing that the wolf's head is there and that he let you into the area behind it."

"He trusts me only up to a point. I worked hard to get him hooked on the fact I know a helluva lot." Taking off her dark aviator glasses, she glanced at Mace. "And when it comes to Native American power, Marston wants to know people with more knowledge than he has."

"Knowledge is power."

"In more ways than one to that old bastard," Jessie growled. "He may look weak and frail, but he's the worst kind of sorcerer. He makes you feel sorry for him. I watched him when he didn't think I was looking, and his hands weren't shaking. But if I was

standing in front of him, they always did. I think he's
conning me, but I'm going to try and con him in turn.
My father dealt with thieves of all kinds and I'd like
to think I learned a lesson from him on how to set
up this kind of sting."

"Marston didn't get where he is without manip-
ulation."

"He's the worst kind of manipulator. And he believes anyone can be bought."

Mace looked down. "That's Macao under us.
Nice place to visit." He knew the small island boasted a rococo-style church as its main historical mon-
ument. The island, which was a Portuguese
possession, had a lot of high-tech casinos. Gambling
was forbidden in Hong Kong, so everyone came to
Macao to drop their money.

"Are you feeling more relaxed now?" he asked
Jessie.

"A little less highstrung, yes." She banked the
helicopter and headed toward Kowloon, which sparkled in the distance. "But I don't want to go back to
a bugged room, Mace. We have too much to talk
about, to plan. We have to figure out how to set this
harebrained sting in motion. *If* it can be put into motion at all!"

Mace touched her shoulder. Feeling the tension,
he said soothingly, "Then let's land this helicopter
at another hotel on Kowloon. Just pick out a helipad

and set it down. We'll have dinner, talk, plan and then eventually make our way back to the Shangri-La. Sound good?"

"Yeah." Jessie gave him a warm look. "You know what? When we first began this mission, I thought you were just baggage, but have I ever changed my mind! I'm not used to this spy type stuff. And I'm really glad you're here, Mace."

He smiled and squeezed her shoulder. "We're a team, Jessie. A good one. Once we land, we'll make some phone calls to Mike and Morgan and see what they can put into motion on this sting of yours. I don't think anyone thought that we might be able to lure Marston onto U.S. soil. That was a brilliant plan."

Grimly, Jessie griped, "Yeah, brilliant. But I'm sure Marston's security check on us will be so deep that I wonder if Mike went far enough to protect our cover."

Jessie took a drink from her glass of chardonnay. They'd landed earlier atop the Intercontinental Hotel, and found this small, quiet lounge off the hotel's main bar area. Relieved to be alone and free from bugs, she'd sketched out different scenarios to Mace, who proved to have a sharp mind for tactics and strategy. Her ideas, as wild and improbable as she'd thought they had been, didn't look so impossible now.

He leaned over the bamboo-and-glass coffee table, a notepad in front of him. "Okay, I want to go
over everything to make sure we've got it right."

Sitting next to him, their arms touching, Jessie
leaned forward to review the information on the
notepad.

"First, Marston believes that Grandmother Ivy
will sell the crystals to him."

"That's right. He didn't blink an eye about that,
Mace."

"So, because he's so obsessed with getting Native
American artifacts that have power—and now we
know why—you've been able to blindside him to a
point. But he still thinks you might be setting him
up. As much as he wants that power, he's going to
wait before he commits to our sting."

Jessie grimaced. "Like I said, I'm really worried
about that part of it. If Marston finds one little piece
of info about our cover out of place, this plan will
die on the vine."

"We'll come up looking like the real deal. You've
already put Mike on notice. Don't worry so much."
Mace smiled. "You're a better undercover agent than
you give yourself credit for. You walked the talk of
a woman warrior for your people today. Even I was
taken in by you in this costume." He gave her an admiring look as he pulled one of her braids.

"And to think, all those years of me and Snake

dressing up to go dancing in Cuzco with those Latino dudes finally paid off." She laughed softly. "Still, Marston's a smart guy, Mace."

Shrugging, he said, "No question. We all have our weaknesses, though. And you've tapped into his Achilles' heel, Jessie. You told him that those crystals are ten times more powerful than the clan totems. That's all he had to hear. He's desperate to keep stealing energy from anything that has power. He wants to stay alive long enough to get some genetic treatment that will turn back the clock on his disease. Desperate people do desperate things."

"Yes, but we need to play it very carefully around him. Sometimes he'd look at me like I was the law coming to get him. Other times, he treated me like a granddaughter. He went from one extreme to another."

"It's his nature to be very careful. And with that in mind—" Mace pointed to the plan mapped out on the notebook "—I'm going to assume that we pass Marston's security and background check. Mike is setting up a Swiss bank account for us. Marston will deposit money there."

"Right."

"And Mike will call Kai Alseoun and Jake Stands Alone Carter to fill them in on this plan."

"She's probably going to balk on this one."

"I doubt it. They want the clan totem back."

"Yes, but they're not going to get the wolf's head back immediately. You and I know we have a real chance to nail Marston. And to take the totem now would only tip him off."

Tapping the pen on the notebook, Mace frowned. "Maybe we need to think outside the box some more, Jessie."

She frowned. "Oh? How? What?"

"You said that there are access doors for the museum help, right?"

"Yes."

"How do you open the access door near the entrance? Is it iris recognition, like the red doors?"

Shaking her head, she said, "No. It's like the door in room three. You need to punch in a code."

"What if…" he turned to her and grinned wolfishly "…we e-mail digital photos of the totem to Mike to get someone to carve, very quickly, a duplicate of the Wolf Clan totem? It could be brought to us by Perseus jet."

Jessica sat up. "Brilliant!" she whispered. "Oh, dude, that is one cool idea!" She could barely sit still. "Swap the fake one for the real one?"

"Yeah, if it's possible. Now, as far as you know, Marston's leaving the totem here, right?"

"Yes. But…" Her voice fell. "I'm supposed to meet him in Asheville to oversee the exchange of crystals."

Mace said, "Don't worry about that. We can manage it."

"What? Me be in two places at once? I don't think so. Marston insisted on cell phone contact with me. He can look at his cell, and if I'm here in Hong Kong trying to find a way into his museum to make the swap, he'll know it."

"No, he won't, Jessie. We can clone your cell phone and Marston will think that you're in Asheville, waiting for him to arrive. No matter how many times he calls, we can create the fake link to fool him. So don't worry about that...."

Excited, Jessie found her mind racing at Mach 3. "Then...I'll get this set up with Marston. First, I need to get back into the museum to photograph the wolf's head."

"Right. I have an idea about that. Since you're supposed to set up a meeting with Grandma Ivy, tell him that she wants a photo of Marston so she knows he's the dude to pass the crystals to. The hard part will be getting him to agree to pose in the room with the Wolf Clan totem."

"Basically, Grandma would be asking for proof and identification."

Mace smiled hugely. "And Marston, for one, should understand why."

Jessie threw her arm around his shoulder and gave him a kiss on the cheek. "Mace, you are *awesome!*"

Absorbing her joy, her womanly strength, he stopped himself from responding as he wished to. Right now, they had to plan like crazy, not get enmeshed in emotional matters, as much as he wanted to. Seeing the happiness sparkling in her blue eyes, Mace allowed himself the luxury of savoring the moment with her.

"Not so fast," he cautioned as she began to review the notes again. "Mike has to find a carver. Someone who can make the imitation *fast*. Because while Marston is winging his way to Canada and then bluffing his way through U.S. Customs and past all the passport officials, we aren't going to be in North Carolina waiting for him."

"No, we'll be here, waiting to trade the fake totem for the real one. According to Mike, there's an extraditions agreement in place between Canada and the U.S. to get Marston. That's why he's afraid."

"That's right." Mace sat up and stretched his shoulders to get rid of the tension in them. "We're playing for high stakes, Jessie. Somehow, you have to get the code numbers for the outer access door. Without it, we have no way in or out of that place. It's airtight, from what I can see."

"Okay, I'll work on that. I know the inner door is 2242, but I'm sure the codes are all different." She wasn't certain how she'd get the info from Marston, but she would. And then it hit her. "Mace! That dream I had on the jet. Remember? The numbers were 2241. Very close to the real ones for his museum." Shaking her head, Jessie murmured, "That's an amazing coincidence."

"So, you'll call him first thing tomorrow morning, after breakfast? We should know a lot more from Mike by that time."

Rubbing her hands together, she whispered, "I'd give anything to get that clan totem back to Kai and Grandma Ivy."

Mace put his notebook away. "I'd give my right arm to nail Marston. This is an unexpected gift to U.S. law enforcement agencies."

Grinning, she said, "What now?"

"Let's call Mike from the helicopter and head home."

Getting up, she gripped his hand. "Let's saddle up, pardner."

Jessie's cell phone was ringing and ringing and ringing. Jerking her head up, she saw that the room was dark. What time was it? Eyes puffy with sleep, she fumbled for the device on the bedstand. She felt Mace move nearby. Throwing off the sheet, she sat up.

"Hello?" Her voice was raspy with sleep.

"This is Mike Houston, Jessie. You need to get dressed and get out of the room so we can talk. Give me a call back?"

"Uhh…yeah, will do. Bye…" She flipped off the cell phone and turned on the lamp. The light hurt her eyes. What time was it, anyway? Rubbing her eyes, she saw from the bedside clock that it was 4:00 a.m.

Groaning, she slid out of bed. Repeatedly, Jessie had to remind herself this place was bugged. "Darling, I need to make a call. I'm going to leave the room to do it so you can keep on sleeping." She saw that Mace was sitting up, the sheet draped around his narrow hips, his hair tousled, eyes drowsy.

"Yeah…everything okay?"

Walking to the bathroom, Jessie called over her shoulder, "Oh, fine. It's just my mother…she loses track of time zones and calls at the weirdest hours, as you know. I'll just jump into my jogging outfit and call her back. Go back to sleep."

Quickly pulling on a white T-shirt and her navy-blue jogging pants, Jessie slid her feet into her tennis shoes. She was still fighting her drowsiness as she left the room, shut the door quietly behind her and headed for the elevators.

The stars were winking overhead when she reached the helipad where their Titan Industries bird sat with chocks around its three wheels. Jessie saw the glimmering lights of Hong Kong across Victoria Harbour. Below, a green-and-white Star Ferry chugged across the dark waters. Flipping open her phone, she selected Mike's number on the speed dial menu.

"Mike? It's Jessie. What do you have?"

"Plenty. Sorry to boot you out of bed so early, but I thought you'd want to know we found a carver. She's from Anaconda, Montana. We got lucky on this one. I didn't tell her anything except that a photo would be sent to me soon and that she had forty-eight hours to make the creation. She said she could do it if it's not too intricate."

Relief sizzled through Jessie. She was wide awake now as she slowly walked around the helicopter. The breeze was humid and smelled of the sea. "It's not intricate. That's great, Mike!"

"Now all you have to do is get that photo asap."

Jessie stopped walking as a meteor flashed across the sky. "Yeah, that's something I'll pursue today, Mike. I have to persuade Marston to let me back in the museum. I don't think it will be a problem, though."

"I've contacted Kai and Grandma Ivy. They know the plan. Plus we're working with the CIA to clone your phone. So everything's in motion here."

"Great. I'm so excited. And scared."

"Stay scared. If Marston has the slightest suspicion you're a spy or trying to manipulate him, your life is worthless. You know that."

Mouth dry, Jessie whispered, "Yeah, I know, Mike."

"We're getting a lot of hits by Marston's security department, checking out your background. So far, so good. They even phoned the university where Mace supposedly graduated, and we rerouted that call to the CIA and confirmed it. So he's doing a very thorough check on you two. Okay, go back to bed."

She laughed softly. "Not now...I'm too damned excited."

Houston chuckled. "Okay, contact me when you have those digital photos to send. And make sure you send them from some Internet café. Do *not* send them from your hotel. You can't trust anyone. Okay?"

"Got it. Out." Jessie pushed the off button and flipped the case closed. As she turned, she saw a dark shape heading in her direction. Heart pounding, she tensed. Who was it?

Mace! A breath exploded from her in relief. His face was deeply shadowed. He wore jeans and a yellow T-shirt with a red Chinese dragon on it. Hair still mussed, he lifted his hand as he drew closer.

"You scared the hell out of me!"

"Sorry, I didn't mean to." Mace ran his fingers through his hair. "What's up? Was that Houston?"

Nodding, Jessie told him everything in a low voice as they stood near the tail rotor of their helicopter.

Mace wearily rubbed his face, which needed to

be shaved. Looking at Jessie, at her braids coming loose, he smiled. "Well, that's all good news."

Jessie dug her toe into the concrete helipad, brows drawn. "The hard part will be getting Marston to sit next to that totem so I can take a photo."

"You're going to have to get the wolf's head from every angle, you realize that? Otherwise, this sculptor won't be able to make an exact duplicate. We don't know who goes through that museum hourly, but we do know the guards are there. And knowing Marston, those guards will have memorized, in detail, what every one of those artifacts looks like."

Rubbing her chin, she muttered, "Yeah…we know he's got twenty-four-hour guard service, but I don't know their duty schedule."

"Do the guards check the catwalk behind the displays? Or do they just do a walk-through of the rotundas?"

Jessie sighed. "I don't know, Mace," she said, giving him a look of desperation. "This spy business sucks. Gimme an Apache helicopter to force some drug dude to turn back, or let me shoot a Black Shark out of the sky. That seems a helluva lot easier than this stuff."

Sensing her worry, Mace slid his arm around her shoulder and drew her near. He wanted to do much more than that, but again, now wasn't the time. No, Jessie had to stay focused. Turning her around to hold her, to kiss her, would be stupid. He wanted her clear on what she had to do, not distracted.

"Come on," he urged gently, "let's get back down to the room. We need all the sleep we can get. If you're tired, you won't think as clearly, Jessie."

"Yeah, yeah, I know that." She fell into step with him, leaning her head against his shoulder for a moment as they walked together.

"Anyone ever tell you that you're good at what you do?" she asked him wryly.

"What do I do?" Mace asked, halting to open the door for Jessie. He saw her looking at him with a new respect in her eyes. That made him feel good.

"What do you call people like you in the CIA? Handlers?"

"Yeah, that's the word."

Jessie stopped in the open doorway, reached up and caressed his cheek. "You handle me real well."

Laughing, Mace said, "No, that's not true. With a name like Wild Woman, there isn't a man alive who would even begin to think he could handle you."

She removed her hand from his cheek. "Oh, you know how to handle me exactly right, Mace. And I don't buy for a second that you don't."

Feeling heat move up his neck and flood his face, he whispered in a husky tone, "Let's talk about this some other time. You need to get ready for Marston."

Chapter 13

"Master Marston awaits you in his study. Please follow me."

Meng, the valet, had met her at the helipad, where Jessie arrived alone. When she had phoned earlier in the day, Marston instructed her to return to Lihua, and Mace to meet with his corporate team specialists at his offices overlooking Victoria Harbour. She and Mace knew that Marston wanted Jessie to himself. Divide and conquer.

That was all right with her, although Mace had looked worried. She was, too, truth be told. She just hoped she could pull this off without Marston becoming wary. Her stomach felt as if a fist was squeezing it. Right now, she'd rather be facing down a Black Shark helicopter.

But she smiled at Marston's assistant. "Of course," she murmured, falling in behind Meng.

The morning was warm. The perfume of flowers—jasmine, Jessie guessed—filled the humid air. Everywhere she glanced she saw gardeners working industriously to keep the grounds around Marston's home immaculate. Already, the tents from the barbecue had been taken down and everything restored to normal. There was no sign of the party that had lasted until dusk yesterday. It was an amazing change, but Jessie knew Marston had the money to hire this brigade of worker bees if that was what it took.

Today, she wore a dark brown skirt of tencil to match her deerskin vest, a white cotton shirt with the sleeves rolled to just beneath her elbows and her comfortable gold buffalo-skin boots. She made sure the fake medicine bag was hanging from her black belt studded with silver conchas and that the small digital camera was in the pocket of her skirt.

As Meng led her to Marston's main house, Jessie began to feel nauseous. It was nerves, she knew. The feeling intensified as she entered the rose-hued Italian marble foyer and ascended the slightly sloping ramp to a dark mahogany door carved with a golden emblem of the sun. Jessie was sure it was real gold, not brass.

"Please go in," Meng told her, opening the door.

"Thanks."

"Ah, good morning, Jessie!"

Robert Marston sat behind a massive desk that was also carved with symbols. She could make out a horse and coyote. He was a coyote, all right. Well, so was she. A bigger, badder one.

Summoning a smile, she waved her hand in greeting and walked across the light-and-dark-patterned parquet floor. *"Netone'xovomohtahe?* How are you?" she asked him in Cheyenne.

His face blossomed with a smile. "Ah! Cheyenne! You speak it beautifully! Come, sit down, Jessie, and tell me what you've found out so far."

She took the offered seat, a chair sumptuously covered in gold fabric and made of mahogany, like his desk. She smiled and said, "I thought you might appreciate our language. Do you know any of it?"

As soon as she'd sat down, a maid silently glided into the room. She placed a tea service next to Jessie on a round mahogany table that had the moon carved on its surface. Jessie watched as the young woman, dressed in a black skirt and white blouse, served Marston, who, she supposed, was dressed down, in a camel-colored blazer, an open-collared white silk shirt and dark brown trousers.

"Oh, I'm a little conversant in Lakota. But not much," he said, watching as the maid poured steaming tea into a pale yellow china cup. "I thought you might have already had breakfast, but there's nothing like hot tea at 10:00 a.m. to make you feel even better. My tea comes directly from Darjeeling. Only the freshest and the best, so please…" He gestured grandly toward the tray.

"Thank you," Jessie said, fixing her own tea that the maid had poured. It was not a favorite drink of hers, but under the circumstances, she wanted to keep Marston amenable to her coming request. If her stomach knotted any more, she felt as if she'd throw up. Not a cool move.

After the maid left, Marston leaned back in his dark leather chair. "So, tell me, you called Grandmother Ivy?"

Sipping the Earl Gray tea, which had fragrant bergamot in it, Jessie said, "Yes, and several things have to fall into place before the exchange. First, she wants to see a photo of you."

"Understandable. She wants to verify that when I show up in Asheville, I'm the right man. I like caution. It's good if all of us are cautious."

Jessie set the cup down on the tray. If only her nerves would settle down! "Secondly, she wants to see the wolf's head totem." Giving a careless shrug, Jessie murmured, "You understand that she doesn't know you from Adam. She requested a couple of photos of you sitting next to the crystal. Plus, she wants to see the condition of the totem."

Jessie pulled the digital camera from her pocket and held it up. "With your permission, I thought I might take three or four shots of you in your museum, beside the display case containing the wolf's head totem. I told her I would take the shots with your permission, and e-mail them to her."

"Does she even have a computer?" he asked in surprise.

Jessie saw the wariness in his eyes. Had he found something on them in his background check? Her heart raced with anxiety.

"No, but the library on the reservation does, and I know the e-mail address for it. What I'll do is take photos today, Robert, and then go back to the hotel and send them to her."

"Don't bother," he said. "You can use one of the computers in my secretary's office." He pointed to a closed door across the room.

Jessica gulped. She was going to send the pictures to Mike Houston! There was no way she wanted Marston to see that e-mail address! What was she going to do? Her mind raced.

"If it's all the same to you, I'd like to use my laptop in our room. I want to crop the pictures and tweak them a little. Besides—" Jessie looked down at the gold Rolex on her left wrist "—I have an appointment to meet my husband in an hour and I don't want to miss it." When Marston gave her a long, hard look, Jessie wanted to gulp again but didn't. What was he going to do?

"Not a problem," he said finally. "And how long will it take Grandmother Ivy to get these photos?"

Knowing that the carver had to have time to replicate the wolf's head, Jessie said, "You know how it is on a res, Robert. Time has no meaning to people. But I'm sure in this case she'll get to the library sooner rather than later."

"Give me an idea?"

"I would say seventy-two hours."

"Very well. And once you hear back from Grandmother Ivy?"

"If she's okay with everything, she'll let me know."

"Whatever she wants, I'll meet it. You have my permission to say yes to whatever she requests."

"Are you sure?"

"My dear, I'm worth so many billions that I've lost count." He gave her a narrowed look. "By the way, I'm sure it's obvious to you that my security department gave approval on you and your husband. So, from my standpoint, I'm satisfied that you are who you say you are."

She had to pretend not to be relieved. "I'm glad

you no longer think I'm the law in disguise setting up a trap for you, Robert." She laughed lightly.

"Do you have that Swiss bank account number? Is she still charging me ten million apiece, providing she's convinced I'm legitimate?"

"Yes, the account could be in place by 5:00 p.m. today. And, yes, Grandmother Ivy said the price on the crystals will be ten million each."

"Excellent," he said.

Jessie held up her camera. Here came the next big test: getting the photos. "Tell me when you're ready for your Candid Camera moment. The sooner I can get these to the library on the res, the sooner you can have those crystals."

As Robert wheeled himself to the entrance of the museum, Jessie noticed two workmen in gray, one-piece cotton suits nearby. The older of the two held a broad broom in his hand. The younger one juggled a bucket, sponges and other window washing equipment in his arms. Both men stopped and bowed deferentially to Marston as he greeted them in Cantonese.

Jessie watched the older workman walk toward the keypad next to the outer door that would allow the men entrance to the catwalk. Quickly glancing to Marston, she saw him position himself so that his iris could be checked for the first door to open.

Glancing back, she strained to see what buttons the old man, who was very slow, pressed. Heart pounding, she couldn't make out the code, but she could tell that the man didn't enter the same four numbers that Marston used to open the access door in room three. Oh, God, how was she going to find out the numbers? Gritting her teeth, Jessie turned and hurried into the museum behind Marston.

"I don't normally have my photo taken anymore," he said jovially over his shoulder.

Stopping at the second red door as Marston cleared security, Jessie said, "You're a handsome man, Robert. Besides, as you know, Grandmother Ivy just wants to make sure no impostors come in your place."

Wheeling his motorized chair through the door, Marston said, "I like that she's careful. I'm looking forward to doing business with her."

Finally, they reached the third room. Jessie tried to hide her distress at the many pipes displayed. Though she dearly wanted to take them all when she and Mace carried out the "swap," it would be impossible, she knew.

She watched as Marston wheeled into position near the crystal. Close by, she heard sounds of the workmen. Peering into another display case, she could make out the two men working on the catwalk. The younger one appeared to be ready to clean the glass case, while a new man, most likely the conservator, carefully withdrew artifacts. Farther down, even though the lighting was low, Jessie could detect the older man slowly sweeping the walk.

"I like things kept spotless," Robert said, waving in their direction.

"Spotless and beautiful," Jessie murmured.

She began to set the parameters on her digital camera. She wanted close-ups. And timing was everything. She had to take four photos, one for each angle of the wolf's head as it slowly turned on the green velvet cushion.

Her hands shook a little. This spy business was terrible on her nerves. "Okay," she said to Robert, "look up." She clicked once, then checked to make sure it was a clear photo.

"A second one?" Again, Jessie timed it. After each of the four shots, she made sure the images were clear. When she finished scrolling through the pictures, she handed Marston the camera. "See if you approve?" Jessie knew Marston wasn't stupid. Letting him look at the pictures was a sign of trust. She just hoped he paid more attention to himself in the photos than the wolf's head totem.

"Thanks." He pushed the buttons to look critically at each photo. "I think I like number three the best."

"Then that's the one I'll transmit. When I'm done, I'll delete all of them."

Handing the camera back to her, he said, "Good. I don't like unauthorized photos of me floating around." He shook his finger up at her. "You know, this is a huge amount of trust on my part, Jessie."

"I understand that," she murmured, turning off the camera and pocketing it.

Looking at his watch, he said, "I have an important phone call scheduled in ten minutes, and must get to my office. I think we're done here."

Nodding, Wild Woman noticed that the workmen had finally come to their side of the display cases. They worked slowly but surely. "Do they ever clean at night, Robert?"

Wheeling himself to the red door, he pressed the button to open it. "Oh, no. At night, this place is off-limits to everyone, including my cleaning crew. The only ones here are my guards."

Walking at his side through the second room, Jessie said, "I would imagine this place becomes like Fort Knox then? Laser beams crisscrossing? That sort of thing?"

"Oh, yes," Robert murmured, satisfaction in his tone. "I don't trust anyone. I've installed state-of-the-art motion detectors, as well."

"Good choice," she declared. The question she couldn't ask was were the lasers and motion detectors in the museum only, or were they installed on the catwalk, too? She hadn't seen the workmen do anything but enter the code to open the access door. Of course, there could be a main console where the lasers and motion detectors could be turned off, but she had no idea where.

Once they reached the exit, Robert held out his hand to her. "I'm running a bit late, my dear. Can you see yourself to the helipad?"

Jessie shook his limp, damp hand. "Of course. I'll call you as soon as I hear from Grandmother Ivy. Expect that to happen in about three days."

"Excellent. Now, if you'll excuse me?" He released her hand, smiled and turned his wheelchair toward the main house. Meng waited for him.

The access door suddenly opened. Jessie turned and saw the younger man, his uniform splotched here and there with water. Her stomach was still in knots and she was sure her blood pressure was arcing up to three hundred about now. Taking a chance, she said, "Oh…excuse me! I accidentally left my camera in the museum. Mr. Marston had to leave sooner than expected to take a phone call in his office, so can you let me back in to get it?" She gave the young man her best pleading smile.

"Uh…you have to see Mr. Marston, madam. I'm not allowed to let anyone in here."

Her pulse bounded and her tone grew desperate. "But I *need* that camera now!"

He stubbornly shook his head. "I cannot do as you request, madam."

"Look, my camera has photos of something Mr. Marston wants. Now, do you want him to be angry because you won't let me back in there to get it? Do you want me to call him on my cell phone here and make a complaint?" She pulled the phone from her pocket and opened it. It was all a bluff.

Frowning, the young man scratched his head. "One moment..." He dropped the sponges he held into the pail of water. Setting the bucket down, he ambled over to the side of the museum. Jessie followed discreetly. The man began to squeeze himself between the building and a tall shrub that nearly reached the roof of the museum.

"What are you doing?" she demanded. "Can't you just open the door?" What the hell was he doing?

"Uhhh...no."

Jessie watched as he fumbled to open a small box on the side of the building. She heard him curse in Chinese before squeezing out of the tight spot.

"One moment, please, madam..."

The old man exited the access door just then. He gave Jessie a confused look and then spoke in Chinese with the younger man. After a brief, sharp exchange, the old man set his broom on the sidewalk and unzipped his upper left pocket. With trembling hands he pulled out a piece of paper and read what was printed on it very slowly to the younger worker, who went back to the box and began punching in numbers. He closed the box and returned to where Jessie still stood, desperately committing to memory the words she'd heard spoken repeatedly.

"You may now go in the front door."

The front door? What about the code for the access door?

"But…Mr. Marston has to show his iris to that gadget over there…" She pointed to the sensor.

The young worker said smugly, "We have disabled the alarms. All you have to do is pull on the door handle and it will open. I will escort you in."

Amazing! "Thanks." Jessie hurried forward, her hands in the pockets of her skirt. Sweat was running down her rib cage as she tried to look cool, calm and detached. What a joke! She felt anything but! Somehow, she had to reach that third room and plant the camera before this dude saw it was all a ruse to get the code.

Hurrying ahead, she was happy to see that the young man didn't try to catch up with her. By the time she reached the third room she was able to quickly place the camera beside a display case before the workman arrived.

"There it is!" she said as he entered. Picking up

the camera from where she'd placed it moments ago, she said, "Thanks so much! I'll leave now."

Bowing to her, he murmured, "You are welcome, madam."

Seated once again in the helicopter, Jessie grabbed a paper and pen from the center console before she even got harnessed up, and rapidly wrote down the words that she'd heard the old man say to the younger worker. Not having a clue about Chinese languages, she had to write the words out phonetically. This was yet another time that Wild Woman wished with all her heart Mace had been with her. He'd have understood the code, and they could disable the museum's entire alarm system at that one box!

After placing the paper in her pocket, Jessie closed the helicopter door. A crewman, dressed in the same garb as the workers at the museum, waited on the helipad. At her command, he removed the chocks from around each wheel. Heart pounding with the thrill of what had just happened, Jessie felt her spirits soar. She'd gotten good photos of the wolf's head totem, and, by a stroke of luck, may have discovered how to disable the security system.

She moved quickly through the procedures of starting up the helicopter. The whine of the engines engaging with the rotor sounded like soothing music to her. As the blades began to whirl faster and faster, she put on her aviator sunglasses, gave the crewman a thumbs-up and began her ascent off the concrete helipad.

Flying back across Victoria Harbour to the Shangri-La, Jessie could hardly wait to show Mace the phonetic words. Would he be able to understand what they meant? Excitement thrummed through her. In a way, this spy business was a quiet kind of combat. Not flashy. Not like her flights in the Apache, stalking druggies trying to fly cocaine out of Peru.

The sky was a deep blue, with clouds gathering to the west. Jessie figured that by late afternoon, they would build into thunderheads that would reach Kowloon and drench the port.

As Jessie set the Titan Industries helicopter on the landing pad on top of their hotel, she hoped Mace was back. She could hardly wait to see him!

Chapter 14

"Well? Does it sound like anything? Or have I screwed up the pronunciation?" Jessie sat with Mace on a flowery couch in the quiet alcove off the main lobby. She'd paced their hotel room for an hour until he arrived back from his meeting in Hong Kong.

Holding her scribbled note, he smiled. "Well, what you don't know is that there are nine levels of intonation to each word in Cantonese."

"Oh gawd…" Wild Woman rolled her eyes. She watched closely as Mace studied her handwriting. "That means you could basically take each of those words I wrote down nine different ways, right?"

"Right. Give me a minute…." He rubbed his brow and focused on the writing.

Jessie could barely sit still as she anxiously clasped and unclasped her hands. Mace looked over at her, smiling.

"Okay, here's my best guess—2241. Similar to the numbers you saw punched in at room number three."

"Really? Wow." And then she snapped her fingers. "Oh, geez! Mace! That dream I had on the jet showed me these *exact* numbers!"

Raising his brows, he murmured, "That's right!" He pulled his notebook from his jacket pocket and flipped to that page. "The numbers you dreamed were 2241. I'm not used to working with a psychic. Pretty impressive."

Grinning broadly, Jessie said, "Bang on, pardner. I'll be damned! That wasn't a dream I had. That was a vision. The wolf's head crystal was giving me information." She shook her head and looked at him, astonished. Mace had an amazed expression, too. "Unbelievable. Well, gosh, I guess that confirms it then. The code must be 2241."

Holding up a hand, Mace cautioned, "Now, Jessie, don't get overly excited about this."

"What are you talking about, Mace?"

He leaned back on the couch, resting an arm along the seat back. Jessie joined him and he curved his hand around her shoulder. Keeping his voice low, he said, "The info you got from the workman and through the vision is valuable but somewhere in Marston's home is a security system monitored by *guards*. Now, we know there is a security desk manned by a guard right as you enter room one of the museum. And we know he or someone else circulates through all three rooms on an hourly basis."

"Okay…" She liked the feel of Mace's body next to hers. How easy it would be to lean over and kiss that very male mouth of his. He looked so darkly handsome in his pinstripe gray suit, pale pink silk shirt and burgundy tie. All business. Very sexy. And very desirable. Cutting off that line of thought, Jessie instead mused about how poorly she'd lived up to her Wild Woman image as a spy. Yes, she was spontaneous as hell, but that could get them into trouble.

"That box located on the outside wall of the museum may disengage the alarms, but it isn't the main control station for the lasers and motion-sensitive equipment he's got installed," Mace was saying.

"Damn." She sat forward, leaning her elbows on her thighs. "And here I thought I'd cracked the case and we were in like Flint to make the swap on that totem."

"We may be yet," Mace said. "On the way back here from my meeting with Marston's cronies, I made a phone call to my station chief in Washington, D.C. He's sending orders for a CIA team that's stationed here in Hong Kong to assist us with breaking and entering Marston's museum without, hopefully, making him suspect anything." Mace continued to debrief her on his meeting with Meng, getting access to corporate executives with their software.

"How many cards do you hold close to your chest, Mace?" She smiled at him, impressed.

He met her smile with one of his own. "In my business, plenty. You've got redundant backups like crazy. Or you hope you do. That three-person CIA team is deep undercover here in Hong Kong. One works for the Chinese telephone company. Another works for the electric company. The third is a computer expert and works for a major Chinese company."

"Wow…"

"They're all Chinese by birth, so they fit in. That's all I know about them at this point. Anyway, my station chief is going to contact them. They will know that we'll need a power outage in order to get into Marston's home. And it can't be just any power failure. The agent at the electric company is going to have to use the computer to deny electricity to the part of Hong Kong where Marston lives long enough for us to gain entry, make the switch and get out again."

"Sounds like a good plan. Without electricity, Marston's museum is no longer impregnable."

"Not so fast…we don't know that. Remember, he's got at least one armed guard in the museum twenty-four–seven. Further, he may have a backup system of gasoline-fed generators that would keep the security grid online and working. We need to check that out before we do anything."

"Oh…with a generator those lasers would still be working, and if we got in, the alarms would sound?"

"Correct."

"This is harder than I thought it would be, Mace." Jessie grinned. "It's a lot easier to push a button and release a Hellfire missile at a target compared to this."

Mace chuckled. "Yeah, that's called straightforward combat. Our kind of combat is very different. Quiet and behind-the-scenes. And it calls for a helluva lot of flexibility and thinking outside the box. The station chief will call me back in about an hour. I'll discuss the options with him and plans will be relayed to the CIA team here in Hong Kong."

"Why can't you talk to this team directly?"

"Need-to-know only, Jessie. If you or I get caught, we can't name them no matter what our captors do to us—drugs, torture or whatever. We can't blow their cover."

Frowning, she said, "I see."

Mace watched as a Japanese businessman walked through the lobby with his wife on his arm. He was followed by five other men with their wives, all of whom stayed a respectful distance behind the first couple. That was the way it was done over here. Power stood alone. The minions walked way behind.

Mace returned his focus to Jessie. "Listen, you need to consider what could happen if we get caught."

"I'm not going to get caught."

Seeing the stubborn set to her lips, he sighed. "This isn't a game, Jessie. It's for real. We want to make the exchange with no one the wiser. But if something goes wrong…those guards of his aren't going to be nice."

"I hear you. And I've thought about it." She flexed her right hand into a fist as she stood up. "I'm sickened at how that bastard treats our ceremonial items. If I can get that wolf's head back, then I'll feel a little better about it."

Mace realized that Jessie lived her life without really looking at what could happen to her in a worst-case scenario. She flew combat daily, yet was impervious, it seemed, to the threat of death. And his heart lurched because he knew in an undercover sting like this, things could go terribly wrong no matter how much the team wanted it to go right.

"Well," he murmured, "we need to coordinate this swap just as Marston is going to meet Grandmother Ivy. I talked to Mike Houston, and he said the plans with Kai and Jake are laid. The FBI will be there, as well, to take Marston into custody."

"We need to coordinate seizure of the money that is intended payment for the crystals. I told Marston we'd set up a Swiss bank account. I need to give him the account number."

Nodding, Mace said, "We have to decide a plan of action on that, clear it with Morgan and Mike, and then with my station chief. He'll then relay whatever the final decision is to the FBI. This is a massive effort among agencies."

"That's what it's going to take to get Marston," Wild Woman muttered grimly.

Easing to his feet, Mace held out his hand to her. "Can I interest you in the California Restaurant on top of the hotel for a late lunch?" He saw her eyes widen. Her smile was real—and for him. Mace felt heat, like sweet, warm syrup, flowing through him. Every day spent with Jessie made him more aware that he wanted to live life again and pursue a relationship of some kind with her. As she slid her fingers into his, Mace wondered if it was possible to fall in love at a time like this.

"Yes, I'm starving for a good green salad! Lead on!"

* * *

Mike Houston called Jessie's cell phone shortly after their lunch. She and Mace had decided to go to the roof, only a few floors above the restaurant, to talk in privacy. Atop the helipad, the breeze was picking up, so Jessie chose a sheltered spot to speak to him.

"We're sending a Perseus team, a man and woman of Chinese heritage, to snoop around Marston's villa to find and disable those gasoline generators," Mike said. "I'm sure he's got them. He's not going to leave millions of dollars' worth of museum pieces unguarded due to a power outage."

"That's great, Mike. Any news on the Swiss bank account?"

"I've been thinking about that," Mike said. "And I have a plan that I'll discuss in a moment with you."

"Okay. What about the crystals? I know Marston will want proof of them. I can see that question coming from him the next time we talk."

"Not a problem. I got Kai and Jake to purchase some large Brazilian crystals from a dealer I know in Virginia. They're working with Grandmother Ivy to place them in the *real* ark. Kai will then photograph them and send the image to you via e-mail. Just make a color copy of it and hand it to Marston."

"Great! Now, what about Marston's money?"

"Well, it's a *lot* of money. I'm sure he's wondering what some elderly medicine woman will do with it all. Grandmother Ivy would probably want to distribute it to her favorite Indian charities."

"Eastern Cherokee? Other nations' charities?"

"All the above. Yes, Marston believes everyone is motivated by almighty greed, but let's tell him that she will put the money to use feeding the poor. After all, elders of any nation are charged with caring for the sick, the hungry and needy. I think that response will raise less of a red flag than an elder so quick to sell her people's sacred crystals. So far, you've been able to convince him that this is no trap, but we need to tread carefully."

"I hadn't thought of this angle, Mike, but you're right. It sounds like good, solid thinking. Can you get me a list of charities to really sell the story?"

"Jenny is sending a list to you by e-mail as I speak. As I said, I've been anticipating that this question would come up, and she researched legitimate charities."

"Great, Mike. I'm excited. It's all coming together."

"Well..." he hedged, "I'm sure Mace has told you this is a complicated operation. Marston could get cold feet at the Canadian border. Or your plan to swap the wolf's head totem could blow up, too."

"How's the sculptor coming along on the fake one?"

"She says another twenty-four hours and it will be ready to go. We're preparing the Perseus team right now. At some point, they'll make contact with you. I'll send you their pictures. The password that you should give them is Red Fox. Okay?"

"Do I get their names?" Jessie asked.

"Yes. Chuck and Andrea Jiang. They're undercover and are a *real* husband-wife team. Like I said, both are Chinese by birth and their cover is that they've come back to Hong Kong to visit relatives, which is true. They do have a lot of family on the island."

"I've committed the names to memory."

"Good. And tell Mace I'm already working with his CIA station chief as well as with the FBI."

"Do you feel like a spider with a bunch of webs?" She chuckled.

Laughing heartily, Houston said, "This is normal stuff for us here at Perseus and Medusa. Spiders spin webs, but in truth, you are the spider manipulating Marston to get him to do what we want."

Jessie looked at her watch, then at Mace. He smiled back at her, causing a warm glow in the region of her heart. "Okay, Mike, once I get that account number and the names of those charities, I'm going to recontact Marston."

"Yeah, let's keep the energy up and moving forward on this. We don't want to give him any downtime to rethink his position. Oh...wait."

Jessie heard him talking to Jenny Wright.

"Great…" Mike murmured. "Kai and Jake just e-mailed a picture of the fake crystals in the real ark box. I'm going to have Jenny send it to you right now."

"Marston will salivate over that photo," she exclaimed. "I can hand him the photo and the Swiss bank account number simultaneously."

"Yep, we're in the flow on this one. Let me know as soon as the deal is struck."

"Roger that."

"This…this is *incredible!*" Marston whispered, holding the color photo of the Ark of Crystals in his hands. He sat behind his desk in his office, the late-afternoon sun slanting through the blinds.

Jessie smiled and sat relaxed in a chair in front of his desk. It was fascinating to watch Marston become excited like a ten-year-old child who had just been handed his fondest wish. He touched the photo, running his fingertips over it again and again.

"So this is what they look like…."

"Beautiful, aren't they?" Jessie had to give Kai and Jake credit. The seven crystals were the required ten inches long and three inches in diameter. They were completely transparent, except for the six-sided point at one end. What intrigued her was the wooden box, which she knew was the real McCoy. Marston honed in on it, as well.

"This box!" He raised his head and pinned Jessie with an awestruck look. "All those fine carvings near the top. Do you know what all these symbols mean? Some of them are strange. I don't recognize them at all."

"No, I don't understand all the symbols, but I'm sure Grandmother Ivy will fill you in if you ask her."

"Oh, my, yes! Phenomenal! I had heard rumors of these crystals, but to see them...my God, they are mind-boggling! I can't believe she'd let them go for any amount of money."

Jessie felt her gut tie in a knot as his tone shifted from unadulterated excitement to suspicion. She tried to look relaxed.

"Understand that the money's not for her. No, she's going to use it to help the Indian people. I have here a list of all the charities that she's asked me to send money to."

"Oh?" Marston sat back and pressed a finger to his chin in thought. "Not that I care, but can I see the list?"

Jessie handed him the information that Jenny had prepared, along with the bank account number.

Marston reviewed the documents, then gave Jessie a measured look. "So everything's set in Asheville?"

"Everything's set," she answered.

"I'm satisfied then." Marston leaned forward to

press the intercom button. His secretary entered the office promptly, almost standing at attention at Marston's desk.

"Mei, see that seventy million dollars, U.S. currency, is wired to the account on this paper. I want confirmation that they've received the money as soon as possible."

"Of course, Mr. Marston." Mei smiled, bowed and took the sheet.

Just like that... Jessie was blown away by the fact that Marston had authorized the movement of seventy million dollars just like that without even a hint of a second thought. She silently thanked Houston for his intervention and wisdom. Marston indeed looked satisfied, and no doubt or suspicion lingered in his eyes.

Keeping the excitement from her voice, she said, "Once I, too, have independent confirmation, I'll let Grandmother Ivy know that you'll be coming for the crystals."

"Excellent," he whispered. Running his fingers gently across the photo once again, Marston whispered, "You know, I can almost feel their power now...."

"They are the most powerful ceremonial tools I have ever seen," Jessie lied.

"Oh, I believe you. I believe you.... And once I've tasted their power, we can conclude our business, my dear."

"I've requested a photo of Grandmother Ivy so you'll know what she looks like."

"Thank you."

"I hope to have it in the next twenty-four hours."

"Excellent, I'll look forward to our next meeting. And I'm assuming you're flying with me to North Carolina?"

Jessica stared in shock at him for one heartbeat. "Oh, no, Robert, I can't! My husband and I have business in Singapore starting the day after tomorrow. I'm afraid I can't be with you." Sweat beaded her upper lip. Did he see it?

"I'm disappointed," he murmured, frowning.

"I am, too, but the whole reason we came here was to attend your party, then fly to Singapore." She saw him weigh her words. *Oh, Great Spirit, don't let him back out now!*

Jessie felt fear lodge in her throat. Marston *had* to go without her. Otherwise, the plan to break into the museum in his absence would be scuttled. This was a two-person raid to get the Wolf Clan totem back. One person couldn't do it all—not with at least one guard on duty.... She flexed her fingers in her lap, wanting to curl them into a ball, but she didn't dare allow her body language to give her away.

With a sigh, Marston said, "Then you *have* to be there to meet me in Asheville, Jessie."

They had prepared for that condition with the

clone of her cell phone. The mission could proceed as planned. Affixing a smile, she said, "No problem, Robert. I'll be there to meet you." And, God willing, she'd be able to make him believe that from a world away.

Chapter 15

"They're here...." Jessie said in an excited whisper as she peered from the small satellite lobby into the main one. Mike Houston had sent the photos of Chuck and Andrea Jiang, the Perseus team carrying the fake wolf's head crystal. To her, they looked like a typical Asian couple; they didn't stand out at all. Spies, she was learning, faded into the woodwork.

When the petite Andrea Jiang spotted her, Jessie waved. Swallowing her excitement, she grinned as they moved through the crowds in the lobby toward her. Chuck Jiang was about five feet ten inches tall and physically fit. Andrea wore her black hair short, which complemented her own trim frame, and expensive designer glasses. The female agent was smiling.

When they were near, Jessie said quietly, "Red Fox."

Chuck nodded. "Correct."

"This way." Jessie gestured to the secluded corner where Mace was standing, hands in the pockets of his dark blue chinos.

There were two couches facing one another across a bamboo-and-glass coffee table. Andrea and Chuck settled into one, and Jessie and Mace claimed the second after introductions were made. Jessie eyed the small leather valise at Andrea's side. She knew the wolf's head was in there, and she was dying to see it. This wasn't the place, however.

Chuck smiled. "Long flight over here. I always hope it'll get shorter, but it doesn't."

Mace smiled. "I know the feeling."

"We've got the goods," Andrea told Jessie, and she gestured to the valise at her feet.

"Great," Jessie murmured. "Where are you staying?"

"At the Penn," Chuck said.

"Penn?" Jessie frowned.

"Oh," Andrea said with a laugh, "sorry. Veteran

travelers to Hong Kong refer to the Peninsula Hotel as the Penn."

"I see...so you're on the island."

Nodding, Andrea said, "Yes, for a lot of reasons."

Chuck looked toward the entrance to the lobby, checking out the people who moved past.

"This is a safe, quiet space," Mace assured them. "Can I get you some coffee?"

"Green tea?" Andrea asked hopefully.

"The health drink," Jessie said, grinning. "I've come to like it, too."

Andrea patted her slender hip. She wore a pale blue tank top with a dark blue, short-sleeved silk blouse, well-worn jeans and sandals. "Listen, I gotta keep in shape and green tea has weight loss written all over it. I drink one or two cups a day."

"That's what I've heard," Mace said, rising. "Stay put and I'll give the waiter our order. Jessie, you want anything?"

It was 11:00 a.m. and she'd already eaten a huge breakfast. "Just coffee, please. Thanks." She took a moment to absorb Mace's imposing presence as he went to search for the waiter. He stood a good head above most of the Asian people she'd seen, with the exception of Meng. That man was Mace's height. And equally dangerous.

The waiter appeared minutes later, and they stopped their patter while he served tea and coffee.

After he left, Jessie got down to business and said, "Mace managed to get hold of the floor plans for Marston's villa from his architect. We have them in our room. When we're done here, we'll make the transfers."

"Right." Andrea leaned forward. "You'll keep the wolf's head crystal replica."

Jessie nodded. "I can hardly wait to see it."

"Don't worry, it's a dead ringer," Chuck said, smiling. "Marston will never know the difference."

Mace also leaned forward. He liked the fact that Jessie scooted closer, their thighs touching. Today, she looked ravishing in a bright red sleeveless tank top that showed off her svelte form. The low-riding white jeans she wore exposed her belly, and he often found himself wanting to run his hand across her midriff to see if her skin was as velvety as he imagined.

"We've got a printout of the area where the gasoline generators are located according to the architect's drawing. There are two below the museum. You need to disable them." Mace frowned. "And you're going to have to climb a very steep slope to get to your mark on Victoria Peak."

Andrea nodded. "We know Hong Kong well, Mace. It's going to be a nasty climb."

"But you can make it in on foot?" Jessie asked.

"Yes," Chuck answered. He took a sip of his tea,

then set the cup down in the saucer on the coffee table. "We packed the usual. Black-spandex outfit, balaclava, night goggles, Kevlar vest. What we plan to do is drain the two generators of gasoline before our CIA mole in the electric company shuts down power to the Victoria Peak grid." Chuck spread his hands in warning. "He can only fool his supervisor for about ten minutes and then he's going to have to restore electricity to that area."

"Which means," Andrea told them, "that you have ten minutes, once the power is off, to get inside the museum, make the swap and get out."

"I've been concerned about what Marston's people will do when they realize the gas generators aren't working," Mace said, frowning.

Andrea shrugged. "I'm sure they have some sort of SOP—standard operating procedure—but none of us know what that is."

Mace gave Jessie a worried look. "And that's the element we can't control."

"The guard in the first room of the museum is armed with a pistol," Jessie reminded him. "I know he'll use it against us if we're detected."

"We assume you have black outfits, night goggles, Kevlar vests here?" Andrea asked.

"Everything but guns," Mace said. It was against the law in China to carry weapons. To get caught with one meant immediate imprisonment on the mainland for a long, long time. Going the diplomatic route to gain permission would have only eaten time they didn't have, so they'd opted to play it safe, which they could no longer afford to do.

"We told Mike Houston to send over weapons on your flight."

"We've got them," Chuck said. "Right now, customs officials are going through the plane." He grinned. "But we have ways of hiding what we need to hide from them. When I get the okay from the pilot, we'll have the box messengered to your room. You can take possession of everything you need."

Andrea sent Jessie a concerned look. "Review with us the mission profile, okay?"

"The most important part of this operation is to make the swap," Jessie said. "We're timing it so that Robert Marston is in U.S. air space when we enter the museum." She looked at her watch. "There's a twelve-hour difference between eastern standard time and Hong Kong time. Plus a day, because of the international date line."

"Right," Mace said, looking to Jessie. "Houston said we need to get Marston's flight itinerary as soon as possible to know when to break in to the museum."

Turning to face Chuck and Andrea again, he added, "The way we've got it planned right now is that I'll stand guard just inside the outer access door, while Jessie runs like hell down that catwalk to room three. She'll make the swap and return to my post. Hopefully, we'll exit from that door and down the side of the slope to a small door we located on the map. This door will take us through that wall."

"From the air we noticed a spot to conceal a car on Victoria Peak's winding road," Jessie said. "We'll be doing some climbing like you, but on the other side of the slope. If everything goes well, we'll rendezvous with you at the airport."

"What if the guard finds you?" Chuck asked.

"We're not interested in killing anyone. We'll use the tranquilizer guns you brought over."

Jessie smiled. "If our luck holds, I swap the wolf's head and we get out of there, all the guards can do is report that there was a break-in, but nothing was stolen."

"Marston could call you at any time, Jessie," Chuck said. "Mike told us they were cloning your cell phone so that he'll think you're waiting for him in Asheville, North Carolina."

Grimacing, Jessie said, "Yeah. I have to keep my cell on me at all times. I'll put it on vibrate so that if he does call me in the middle of our swap operation at the museum, I can answer him."

"That will be something," Chuck said, laughing. "I can see it now. You're sneaking down the catwalk to make the swap and Marston calls."

"I'm hoping that doesn't happen," Jessie said. She picked up her coffee and took a sip. "If it does, I'll make the call short and sweet. We'll have ten minutes of no electricity, so I'll have to move and talk fast."

"Don't count Marston out," Chuck warned. "He's going to want assurances that you're in North Carolina waiting for him."

"Oh, I don't underestimate him at all."

"Well," Andrea said with a smile, "the next step is to ensure that Marston has sent the money to the Swiss bank account, right?"

"Yes," Mace answered. "Jessie was with him when he made the request. He's supposed to call to let her know he received confirmation, so that she can independently confirm it. They're going to meet again at his villa today. She has a photograph of Grandmother Ivy to give him."

"At your meeting with Marston will you figure out a time and date to meet him in Asheville, Jessie?" Andrea asked.

"I suspect so," she answered. "He made that a condition of our deal."

Chuck said, "So, once this swap has taken place and we're all at the Perseus jet, the next stop is home?"

"Yes," Mace murmured. "You should have the Perseus crew ready to take off immediately, so they need to do their customs and passport clearance with the Chinese officials before that."

"Right," he agreed. "Okay, Jessie, it looks like your meeting with Marston is the next step in our joint mission."

"My dear, here is the proof of my money going to the bank account you designated."

Marston had invited Jessie to lunch in an octagon-shaped alcove in his villa, with the view of Victoria Harbour spread out below them. The table was gaily decorated with a red tablecloth and pink roses in a crystal vase.

Smiling, Jessie took the proffered paper. "Thanks, Robert."

"I'm very curious," he murmured, taking a bite of his carrot-and-apple salad.

Her pulse sped up a bit. "Oh? About what?"

"As I understand it, the Ark of Crystals is the hub of the Eastern Cherokee people. Remind me again why Grandmother Ivy would sell it to me?"

"Grandmother Ivy is a realist, Robert. As I told you, she felt that the amount of money she asked for would do more good to lift her nation and others out of poverty than keeping the crystals. She's progressive and her heart is in the right place for her people."

Obviously pleased, Robert said, "Medicine men

and women are charged with the spiritual health of their people, so her explanation rings of authenticity to me. Besides," he said as he buttered his sourdough bread, "it's so much more noble than plain greed."

A maid entered then with the main course, a savory beef Stroganoff.

"I worry about one thing," he said, looking across the table at Jessie.

She spooned several dollops of sour cream onto her noodles, attempting to act normal despite his probing questions. "What?"

"Well, all things being equal, and not that I doubt Grandmother Ivy and her intentions, but...what stops her from giving me fake crystals?"

Jessie maintained her composure and her smile as she added salt to her meal. "You're a man who knows energy, Robert. I'm very sure you'll be able to tell in a heartbeat if they are real or not. From what Grandmother Ivy said, the crystals are very hot to hold. They get warm very quickly and make your hands tingle." Shrugging, she took her fork and twirled some noodles around it. "Ultimately, you have to be completely satisfied with the crystals or you don't pay a dime. Everyone just walks away."

"Somehow," Robert murmured, chewing a piece of beef, "I feel this elder would rather feed her people now. The whole thing feels legitimate to me."

"Good. It should."

Raising his head, he said, "So, the only thing left is for me to fly to North America."

"I'm scheduled to take off this evening on an EVA flight from here to Taiwan and then on to Los Angeles," Jessie said. "From there, I'll pick up a domestic carrier to Asheville."

"Which one, my dear?"

A cold shudder went through Jessie. She continued to chew her food. After swallowing it, she said, "I'll fax over my flight itinerary. I think you should arrive the same day I do. I have planned to be there midmorning in Asheville. I've asked Grandmother Ivy, her granddaughter and grandson to meet us at roughly 1:00 p.m. East Coast time."

Nodding, Robert said, "Very good. As soon as we get done here, I'll shoo you off and have my secretary get my jumbo jet prepped for takeoff. I do wish you could fly there with me, though."

"I'm sorry, that's impossible," Jessie said. "Since I won't be accompanying my husband to Singapore, I agreed to a three-hour stopover in Taiwan to take care of other business for Mace. And—" she blotted her lips "—I have to meet our business manager in Los Angeles. No, there's too much going on and I have to make too many stops. I'm sure you understand. You have to make every hour count when you run a multimillion-dollar global business."

Snickering, Robert said, "Oh my, yes, I do, my dear."

Though she was relieved that Marston bought her story, Jessie had one big problem: there was no way she could be on that EVA flight. Had Mace been able to plug that hole in the dike?

"What have you done to get a double for me on that EVA flight tonight?" Jessie demanded as she met Mace on the roof of the hotel after landing the helicopter.

He took her by the arm and led her away from the concrete helipad, where two crewmen were busy tying down the blades and putting chocks around the bird's wheels.

"We've got a CIA field agent who is going to wear a black wig and carry your passport. She will board that flight in your place, so don't worry."

"What if Marston has someone looking for me on that flight?"

"That's covered, too. I'll take you to the airport. You'll check in and proceed to the departure lounge. You'll be wearing your hair down and dark glasses. Our field agent is your height, with similar features. You'll go to the bathroom just before they call for first class boarding. In the restroom the agent will hand you carry-on luggage, then leave to take your place, wearing an identical suit of gray wool with a cream-colored tank top and dark brown leather loafers. Meanwhile, you will get rid of the wig and change into the new clothes in the bag. You'll ditch the bag in the wastebasket when you're done. When you come out of the bathroom, you'll be blond and wearing jeans, jogging shoes and a tank top."

"Amazing," Jessie said.

Mace opened the door for them to exit the roof. The temperature was in the eighties and the humidity was high, so he was glad to get into the air-conditioned comfort of the hotel. As they walked toward the elevator, he slipped his hand into hers. There was no one around, but that didn't matter. Gently pulling her to a stop, he placed his hands on Jessie's shoulders. The surprise and pleasure in her eyes made him smile.

"Listen, this could get rough," he said huskily, his fingers caressing her small, proud shoulders. "And I've been thinking a lot the last couple of days."

"Uh-oh," Jessie teased, resting her hands on his upper arms. She felt his muscles tense as she slowly massaged his biceps. Smiling up at him, she whispered, "And?"

"And so…" The elevator bell rang. The doors opened. He didn't move. She didn't, either. The doors closed.

"My past…I'm at peace with it now, Jessie. Ever since you crashed into my life, I've been seeing things differently. Through new eyes."

"Maybe...with hope?" she whispered. His mouth was so damn inviting. Well, she didn't have the name Wild Woman for nothing. Sliding her arms around his neck, she drew him down so she could reach his mouth. "Show me, Mace," she whispered against his lips, licking the lower one with her tongue.

Life was to be lived! Jessie had found that out a long time ago. She moved her hips provocatively against Mace's narrower ones. He wrapped his arms around her in response, and she liked the fact that she was plastered to him as he backed her into the wall. His mouth was strong, urging her lips open even more. Smiling beneath his mouth, Jessie drank him in hungrily. Oh! Yes! He was a helluva kisser! There was no wasted motion about Mace's onslaught. It was easy to surrender to his power, his maleness. The chaotic breathing, the pounding of his heart—all conspired to make her savor him even more. Feeling the hardness of him grow against her belly, she nipped at his lower lip. He nipped hers back and she laughed huskily.

"I like the way you kiss," she whispered wickedly, and she felt him smile.

"You taste like strawberries and cream."

"Dessert at Marston's..."

The moments melted away. Jessica liked being pinned against the wall next to the elevator. Breathing hard, she continued to move suggestively against his hips until he finally groaned and began to release her.

"Too much?" she teased in a husky tone, giving him a look that told him she wanted to go all the way with him.

Groaning again, Mace nodded. He gripped her shoulders and gave her a slight shake. "Now I know where you got your name, Wild Woman."

"Oh, you haven't seen anything yet," she promised with a smoky laugh. "I'm being a good girl under the circumstances."

Caressing her cheek, Mace grew serious. "Listen to me, Jessie…I *want* to know you after this mission. I'm serious about you. I'm not playing games or being fake."

Touching her lips, she murmured, "That wasn't a fake kiss."

Mace shook his head. "No, I'm not that kind of guy. And you aren't that kind of woman. I've been around you enough to know that much."

"And you want to know if I want you around after we pull off this mission?"

"Yeah, I do."

Wild Woman closed her eyes as he pressed his open palm against her cheek. How natural it felt to nuzzle against it. Giving his hand a quick brush with her lips, she opened her eyes. "I play for keeps, Mace. It's been a damn long time since I had a serious relationship with a man, but this isn't about primal need." Reaching up, she ran her fingertips across his lower lip. "I want the right to know *you,* on every level. I know we can't do anything here, but mark my words, the first time we're together after this mission, it's open season, guy. And you're fair game…."

Chapter 16

It was time. The predawn sky was cloudy, the stars blotted out and the smell of approaching rain heavy in the air. Far out on the South China Sea, flashes of lightning broke the darkness. Hidden in the bushes Jessie lay quietly on the slope just below the museum. Right now, Robert Marston was in Toronto and getting ready to fly to North Carolina. The cell phone was in her right pocket, on Vibrate. If he called—and Jessie knew he would because he'd done so twice during the last three hours—she had to answer it, no matter at what stage she was in the swap. So far, the double ruse was proceeding smoothly.

Tonight, thank goodness, she didn't have to wear that stupid wig. Hidden beneath the black balaclava she wore was her natural blond hair with its dyed red streak. The only thing that could be seen were her eyes. Mace was lying next to her. Both of them were flat on their bellies on the slope. Everything looked a grainy green because of their night goggles. They each wore headsets hooked over their left ears, the microphones very close to their lips. These walkie-talkie devices would keep them in touch when they were separated.

Jessie's heart was beating fast in her chest. Adrenaline. Oh, yeah, she recognized that rush. She got it every time she spotted a Black Shark, after which a deadly game of sky chicken would ensue.

Sweat dotted her brow. She rubbed the dampness with her black-gloved hand and felt Mace shift.

"Nerves," she whispered.

He nodded and gently placed a hand over hers, giving her fingers a squeeze. Mace seemed to be telling her that she was moving around too much.

Jessie nodded to let him know she got it. Squeezing his fingers in response, she took in a long, steadying breath. She wanted to get on with this operation! Not lie here like a rug against the earth. Still, she knew the waiting was necessary. When Mace released her fingers, she peeled back the black nylon over her watch to check the glowing green dials. At 0215 the mission would begin. The CIA mole working in the electric company would shut down the grid. All lights, movement sensors and lasers in and around the museum should be snuffed out.

Somewhere out there in the darkness, Chuck and Andrea were already draining Marston's generators. They were hooked up to the same frequency on their walkie-talkies. Not once, other than a beep to announce their arrival at the generators, had a sound been made or a word spoken. Mace had impressed upon Jessie that silence was more than golden on a mission like this. It was mandatory. Noise could get someone killed.

That thought stilled Wild Woman completely. They had another ten minutes before the power grid would go down. A sharp beep in her ear told her that the Perseus team had completed the job. The generators that would normally feed electricity to the museum during a blackout were now drained of fuel. *Good!*

Compressing her lips, she lay there, waiting, wildly aware of her role on this mission. Not for the first time, she realized that she didn't really like this cloak-and-dagger shit. Oh, the night goggles were essential for this kind of work, but the sweat pooling around her eye sockets where the soft rubber of the scopes pressed against her face was driving her crazy. The goggles were a pain in the ass as far as she was concerned. No, Mace and people like him could have this kind of work. It wasn't for her. She'd rather be up in the air. At least there she had a three-sixty view of everything going on.

Yet, as Jessie looked at her watch to see that they had five minutes more to wait, she understood clearly that if this mission hadn't been mounted, she'd have never met Mace.

Closing her eyes for a moment, she allowed herself to remember that indelible kissing session next to the hotel elevator. Oh, the man could kiss! *Awesome! Double and triple awesome!* She wanted much more than what was available right now. And judging from the burning look in his eyes after they'd kissed, her hips grinding demandingly into his, he wanted a helluva lot more, too.

That was good, because Jessie was going to make damn sure she got thirty days leave from BJS after this little walk in the park in Hong Kong. She'd earned it. She knew it would put a strain on their flight resources in Peru, but, dammit, she wanted a *life* again! And she wanted to explore one with Mace.

She felt him tense. It was nearly time. Mouth dry, her heartbeat skyrocketing, Jessie prepared herself. In a knapsack on her back was the fake totem. It was well packed so it couldn't break. Unless, of course, she fell directly upon it or took a hit from a bullet.

Jessie felt Mace slowly rise to his hands and

knees. That meant it was less than a minute before the grid would be pulled off-line. She mimicked his movements. Heart thundering, Jessie felt adrenaline pouring through her veins. Her black spandex outfit and Kevlar jacket didn't breathe as well as she'd hoped, and she felt like one giant puddle.

She watched the slope, a tranquilizer gun by her side. Fortunately, there were no guards outside. That was good. They knew there was at least one guard inside, in room one. What he would do when the lights went off and no generator kicked in, Jessie didn't know. No one knew. He was the loose cannon, and he was armed with a pistol. She had no illusions about what he would do if he saw them. He would shoot. Marston had told her as much.

Terror sizzled through Jessie. Why hadn't she told Mace how she really felt about him? That she thought she was falling in love with him? She'd censored those words. It had been too soon. Too much else was going on. Now, as she pulled herself up into a crouch, the toes of her boots digging into the damp soil, hands pressed on the earth in front of her, she was sorry she hadn't told him. The possibility of him being hurt, maybe killed, scared her. Gulping, she saw the lights above them suddenly go out. The museum was drenched in darkness.

Without a word, they raced up the slope. The brush slapped at her legs, her face. Jessie pumped her arms as hard as she could to run abreast of her partner. As they topped the slope, she headed to the corner of the museum near the access door, her tranquilizer gun ready in case the guard came out. Right now, he was probably waiting for the generators to kick in. Mace had run directly to the control box on the side of the museum to punch in the code.

She heard a click. Instantly, she leaped to her feet and raced for the access door. *Please, let it open!* Her fingers slid shakily around the doorknob and twisted. The knob turned. Relief tunneled through her. She slipped through the door onto the catwalk. Mace followed right behind her. Neither said a word. They each knew what they had to do.

Jessie's heart was pounding so loudly in her ears as she raced down the catwalk that it was impossible to hear what the guard inside might be doing.

She'd reached the curve around the second room wall when her cell phone suddenly vibrated.

Oh, damn! She slid to a halt. Yanking off the balaclava and then her glove, she quickly dug into her pocket for the phone. Breathing hard, she pushed her night goggles up to her brow and wiped the sweat from around her eyes. *Hurry! Hurry!* Hands shaking badly, Jessie flipped open the case. The bright blue light showed the name of the caller: Marston. Her heart slamming into her ribs, she pressed the series of buttons to signal the satellite to show a mirror cell position of Asheville, North Carolina.

Hurry! She saw the signal blink. It was on! Pressing the button, she held the cell phone to her ear.

"Hello…"

"Hello, Jessie. This is Robert."

"…Yes…Robert. What's up?"

He laughed. "You're breathing hard."

"I'm in the middle of a four-mile jog, Robert." It was around 10:00 a.m. on the East Coast, which made it plausible.

"Staying fit, I see. I'm just checking in again. I wanted to let you know we've just entered U.S. air space, heading for Asheville. In another three hours, we should be landing there."

"That's great…now…if you don't mind, I have two more miles to finish. Today is a big day and…I want to be alert. Okay?"

Laughing, he said, "Of course, my dear. I'll see you soon…."

"Goodbye, Robert." *Bastard!* Flicking off the cell phone, Jessie jammed it back into her pocket, then zipped it closed. How many minutes were wasted? She keyed her hearing. Nothing. What was the sentry doing? Calling for help? Walking through the museum with a flashlight and gun drawn? The scenarios, none of which were good, filled her with fear.

Readjusting her night vision goggles, she ran down the smooth catwalk toward her objective.

There! Jessie was breathing hard as she rounded the turn for the third and final room. Her gaze sought out the wolf's head crystal. When she spotted it, she sprinted to the display case.

Shrugging off her backpack, she carefully laid it at her feet and with trembling hands unzipped it. Getting down on both knees, she opened it wide, and as carefully as possible, unwrapped the fake totem. It was beautiful. The same size, the same quality of crystal. Amazed by the resemblance, Jessie got to her feet to make the switch.

What was that? Turning, she looked to find the source of the noise she'd heard but saw nothing. Breathing raspily, she hauled open the door of the display just enough to reach the wolf's head crystal. Sliding her fingers around the real totem, she felt an instant prickle and heat arc into her fingers and then her hand and wrist. Amazed, she pulled the wolf's head out, then slipped the fake one into the case, setting it gently on the cushion. To Jessie, it looked exactly the same.

She heard another noise, like a door opening and closing. The guard? Was he moving through the rooms, checking them out? More than likely. Heart rate climbing, Jessie shut the display case door. Dropping to her hands and knees, she very carefully wrapped the real wolf's head crystal in two huge, fluffy terry-cloth towels. Sliding the bundle into her pack, she zipped the bag shut. As quickly as she could, she shrugged the backpack into place, then snapped the waist strap and a second strap just above her breasts. Under no circumstances could the precious crystal be broken!

Jessie got to her feet and through the display case saw a guard flashing a strong beam of light around the room. She gasped softly and went flat on her belly on the catwalk. Laying her head down on the cool concrete, she rolled on her side and quietly pulled the tranquilizer gun from its holster.

Jessie knew the guard couldn't get to her unless he went through the access door. She saw the beam comb the wall above where she lay. The base of the glass display case was wood, so the guard couldn't see her. She wasn't visible to anyone—unless they came around the corner of the catwalk and found her lying there.

Blinking her eyes, which were stinging with sweat, Jessie waited. Would the guard come through the access door? Would he check the catwalk? Gripping the handle of the tranquilizer gun, she strained her ears once more, barely able to hear his footsteps on the marble tile inside the room. She could see, however, that he seemed to be moving the flashlight beam across every last damn artifact. Wanting to get the hell out of there, Jessie sizzled with impatience and near panic.

She heard a sharp ping in her earpiece. *Oh, no!* That signal meant Mace had encountered trouble! Swallowing hard, she got to her hands and knees and crawled quietly toward Mace's position. The concrete was hard, her knees taking brutal punishment. But as long as she kept below the display cases, the guard could not see her.

What had happened to Mace? He was guarding the outer door, the only way on and off of this catwalk. She knew she couldn't say a word. If she did, the guard might hear her. Moving silently and swiftly, Jessie reached the end of room three.

She heard gunshots! Far ahead. The sound of gunfire echoed sharply through the catwalk area. *Damn!*

"Guards, four of them!" Mace rasped.

Jessie froze for a moment. What to do? What to do? More gunshots!

Suddenly, the access door burst open behind her. The guard came running along the catwalk, pistol drawn. He saw her!

Jessie was still on her hands and knees. She straightened abruptly to aim the tranquilizer gun at the startled man. He was young and strong, probably six feet tall.

Everything seemed to move in slow motion. The guard gave a cry and aimed the nose of his gun at Jessie's chest. They fired simultaneously.

A bullet hit the center of her Kevlar jacket, the force slamming her backward several feet. She felt a sharp, burning sensation between her breasts as she landed on her left side on the cement. She'd twisted to avoid landing on her back and breaking the wolf's head crystal. Lying there, stunned for a moment, she held on to the gun and took aim as the guard fired at her again.

This time, the bullet ricocheted off the catwalk railing. Eyes huge, Jessie managed to raise herself to her knees. Her entire chest hurt. Breathing was painful. She watched as the guard tried to pull the dart from where it had struck him in the neck, near his left collarbone. He was moving backward, flailing, still firing as he went.

Bullets buzzed around her like angry hornets and she flattened once more against the catwalk. The guard gave a final cry and crumpled to the ground, the pistol falling from his hand.

Scrambling to her feet, Jessie ran to the access door and shut it. It hurt like hell to breathe! Returning to the guard, who lay unconscious, she picked up his gun, tucked it in her belt, then sprinted toward the outer door.

Jessie could hear more gunfire.

"I've got the crystal!" she shouted into her mouthpiece. "I've neutralized the guard. Give me a situation report."

"Four guards," Mace rasped. "Two have me pinned inside the door. Two entered the museum. We're trapped!"

Damn! "Can we get out?"

"No!"

Her mind spun with options. To her knowledge, there were no other exits from the museum. Robert Marston had made his baby foolproof to thieves, that was for sure.

Skidding to a halt, Jessie began to search for another way out. Peering over the railing of the catwalk, all she could see was earth. Smooth, sculpted earth sloping downward to the curved outer wall of the building. No exits. Nothing! Breathing in gulps, she felt sweat running down her face as she listened for guards approaching behind her.

More gunfire! Mace was in deep trouble.

No! Suddenly, Jessie wanted to live as never before. In desperation, she sprinted down the catwalk toward Mace.

She was passing the second room when a door flew open. Two menacing-looking guards carrying AK-47s leaped out onto the catwalk.

Jessie nearly shrieked. She had had no idea there was an access door in room two. Had she missed it?

Holding the tranquilizer gun in both hands, she dropped to one knee and fired at them as they lifted their rifles to kill her.

Chapter 17

Shots echoed around the catwalk. One bullet whizzed so close to her ear, she swore she felt the wind from it. Flattening, she watched the sentries, with looks of surprise on their faces, crumple to the floor, their pistols clattering uselessly from their hands. The darts had hit their marks.

Breathing hard, she leaped to her feet. "Mace! What's happening? Talk to me!"

She heard his raspy breathing. Tensely, Jessie waited at the open door that led into room two.

"I've still got two guards shooting at me from outside the access door. There's nothing I can do but hold them off. We're trapped."

Stepping into the museum, Jessie whispered, "No, we aren't. There's a secret door into the second room! I just tranquilized two guards. I'm moving forward into room one. I'll sneak outside and try to get a bead on those guys. Just keep them occupied for about three minutes?"

"Roger. Be careful...."

It was completely dark in the first room. She looked apprehensively at the security desk, but was relieved to find no one there. Tranquilizer gun in both hands, she quickly skirted the wall toward the front doors, which were wide open. That was good!

Keeping low, she saw movement through her goggles. Yes, there were two guards outside, training their weapons along the museum wall.

Her mind was working in triple time. What if someone had called Marston about the break-in? She'd be very surprised if he wasn't immediately alerted. Assuming he had been contacted, she worried about his reaction. He was still in the air, over U.S. territory. Hearing about this, he could turn around and head back to Canada. A part of her cursed what had occurred here. Still, even if Marston got away and flew back to Hong Kong immediately, they had the real wolf's head crystal. And that was all that really counted.

Looking at her watch, she realized nine minutes had passed. That meant they had one more minute left before the electricity came back online, flooding this place with light and exposing them. Wiping the sweat from beneath her eyes with her gloved left hand, she crouched near the museum entrance. The sentries were completely focused on Mace, inside the access door. They never saw her catlike movements.

Jessie stood up and calmly took a bead on each of the guards. Both turned, wild looks in their eyes, then fell unconscious to the ground.

"Get out here! The guards are down! We've got less than thirty seconds before the lights come back on! Hurry!"

Mace ran through the now-empty doorway, and together they raced full speed to the slope.

Jessie landed squarely on her butt as she slid down the side of the hill. Bushwhacked by twigs and branches, she tried to protect her face with an upraised arm. Breathing hard, she finally fell forward, landing on her hands and knees, rocks, dirt and debris scattered all around her. Gasping, she surged again to her feet. Mace was just behind her. They continued running down the slope. Just as they reached the car, which was concealed in thick foliage by the roadway, the lights flared back to life high above them. Mace had the keys and pressed the button to unlock the Bentley. Hurriedly, Jessie opened the front door on the passenger side and gently placed the knapsack containing the wolf's head on the floor. Hurrying to the trunk, she quickly shimmied out of her black one-piece spandex suit. Mace was ahead of her and already climbing into his black chinos. His chest was bare and gleaming with sweat. Breathing unsteadily and grimacing as she hauled herself out of the Kevlar vest that had saved her life, Jessie felt a sharp ache in the upper part of her chest. Automatically, she ran her fingers across that area. No blood. Just a lot of unrelenting pain, which she ignored for now.

She put on her white silk tank top, threw on a flowery red-and-yellow blouse and a pair of chocolate-brown silk slacks. After shoving her feet into a pair of sensible loafers, she slammed the trunk shut. Mace was rushing to the driver's side.

Jessie looked above and saw nothing. No sounds either. Not yet. The tranquilizer darts would render the sentries unconscious for at least ten minutes. *Hurry!*

She got into the car and quickly pulled the seat belt into place. "Let's go!" she told Mace.

"I'm on it!" The Bentley roared to life, and Mace sped away from their hiding place to head directly for the Hong Kong airport.

Wiping the sweat from her brow, her heart pounding in her chest, Jessie looked over at Mace. He was focused entirely on the twisting, winding road that led down from Victoria Peak. At this time of morning, there was little traffic. Below them glimmered the lights of Hong Kong. Clutching the knapsack in her lap, she whispered, "We did it."

"So far," he growled. Giving her a quick glance, he said, "You okay?"

Nodding, she wiped her mouth. "I'm dying of thirst. I musta sweated ten pounds off in there. Damn, those guards came in unexpectedly...."

"You took them down, though."

Jessie hunted for and found a bottle of water. She uncorked it as the Bentley swayed and swung down the road. In a few minutes, they'd be off the mountain and on the expressway. Drinking deeply, she quenched her thirst.

"Want some?"

"Yeah, in a minute." Mace glanced' at her again. Her blond hair was mussed and flattened against her skull. "You look pale. Are you sure you're all right?" His gut said something was wrong, but he didn't know what.

"Yeah, yeah, I'm okay." Jessie touched her upper chest lightly with her fingertips. "I took a bullet to the vest right here."

His heart plunged. He stared at her for a moment, then returned his attention to the task of driving. "Are you wounded?" God, please don't let her be!

"No...the skin's not broken. The Kevlar did its

job. Where the bullet struck, my chest stings and burns like hell." She laughed. "I bet I'll have one helluva bruise there in a few hours."

"You will," Mace promised her grimly. They were on the expressway now. He had to watch his speed. This was not the time to get a ticket from a cop.

"Oh?"

"Yeah, I once took a bullet to the vest...."

Mace followed the English signs for the airport. He finally got on Garden Road, which led to Queens Road. From there, it was several miles to the Western Harbour Tunnel that would get them off the island. In another forty minutes, if all went well, they'd be at the airport.

"Marston..." Jessie groaned unhappily. "He's got to know of the break-in, Mace. We've blown it, dammit."

"Yeah, I thought about that, too. I'm sure one of those security guards had a cell phone and made a couple of calls." He wiped the beaded sweat off his brow. "That's probably why we had so many guards show up."

"What nearly got me killed was not knowing there was a secret entrance to the catwalk from that second room. I never saw it."

"Don't worry about it. You did a great job, dropping those guards."

Taking the Iridium satellite phone out of the glove

box, she said, "I'm placing a call to Mike Houston. He needs to know we got the wolf's head crystal."

"Yeah, at least we made the exchange…." Mace wanted Robert Marston. He tightened his hands on the wheel and drove the Bentley toward the next step in their escape route: the highway spanning Tsing Yi Island.

He listened to Jessie's low, husky voice as she quickly relayed the news to Houston. Mace's heartbeat wouldn't settle down. Jessie had been hit by a bullet!

The highway was well lit, with little traffic, and he kept the cruise control at the maximum legal speed. Had any of the guards seen the Bentley drive away? Mace didn't think so, but he hadn't taken any chances. Before the mission he'd smeared mud on the license plate so no one could read it and call the police. Just in case.

The lights were like a sulfur necklace strung out on the flat, wide expressway. In no time, they'd crossed the island of Tsing Yi. Another undersea tunnel would take them to Lantau Island. From there, they'd take another highway to the small island that held the new airport.

"Okay, Mike, we'll let you know once we're in the air. Out." Jessie opened up the knapsack and gently placed the Iridium phone near the well-wrapped wolf's head totem. She glanced over at Mace's set face. His mouth was grim, his brows drawn down. This was the man she'd fought side by side with. He'd protected her back, and she his. Reaching out, she slid her fingers along his darkly haired arm.

"You're one helluva warrior in a fix," she murmured. The moment she touched Mace, she saw the line of his mouth soften slightly. It made her feel good that her touch affected him so easily.

"I was worried, Jessie. About *you.*"

"I was fine," she said. Removing her hand, she placed it back on the knapsack. "I was worried about *you* out there."

"Well, it's not over yet," Mace murmured. "The Perseus jet is waiting for us."

"We're right on time," she said, looking at her watch.

"Once we get to the airport, I'll drop you off at the freight hangar where the jet is parked. We can change quickly, then I'll drop this Bentley off at the lease office."

"Got it."

"We'll have to get through customs. One of the officials will come on board the plane, check our passports, ask us if we have anything to declare and then leave."

"Well, we do have something to declare, but they aren't gonna know it."

Jessie knew the danger wasn't over—yet. But she

was getting shaky. The adrenaline surge was dissolving into her bloodstream. If anyone got to the customs officials, they could hold the plane and everyone on board as prisoners. She and Mace would be going nowhere but to a Hong Kong jail. That terrified her. Jessie couldn't even begin to think of being in a prison. Tightening her hands on the knapsack, she muttered, "I've never been more anxious to get into the air. Right now, I can hardly wait...."

The Perseus airbus symbolized freedom to Jessie. Painted black with big white letters that read: Worldwide Freight on the side, the aircraft pretended to be a freight hauler to mask its true activities. As she boarded, one of the three-person flight crew, a female navigator, greeted her. The woman was about Jessie's height, with short red hair and freckles across her nose and cheeks. Jessie guessed her to be in her early thirties. She wore a uniform of black slacks and crisp white short-sleeved blouse with black shoulder boards, a gold stripe across each.

"I'm Karen Harcourt. Welcome aboard, Jessie."

Smiling as she entered the cabin, she said, "Thanks, Karen."

"Got the goods?" The woman held out her arms.

Handing over the knapsack, Jessie said, "Handle with care?"

"Oh, you betcha we will. Follow me? We have a doctor on board and she needs to check you over real quick. Once Mace gets here, we'll call customs to come and search us after they've checked our passports."

Looking around, Jessie noticed that the huge plane had a lot of space for cargo instead of seats. And there were plenty of bulky loaded pallets stowed away under nylon netting. What few seats she saw were in the forward cabin near the cockpit, where a blond woman and a dark-haired man were going through the preflight ground checklist. "Okay...."

In a kitchen area toward the rear of the plane, Karen pulled out a bin with soda cans in it. Removing several rows of beverages, she gently pushed the knapsack to the rear, then replaced the soda before closing the bin.

"The customs routine is straightforward," she said. "Three agents come aboard. They open doors and drawers, look at passports, ask what we've got, and then we're off!" She gestured toward the front of the plane. "Come on, Dr. Gail Carswell is waiting for you. It's SOP to check out all people after a mission."

"Sounds good to me." Following the navigator, who seemed cheerful and unafraid, Jessie felt some of her tension bleed away. She was worried about

Mace. Oh, she knew he could take care of himself, but questions still nagged at her. Had the guards seen them? Called in the theft?

As she followed Karen, she heard voices. Turning, she saw that Chuck and Andrea Jiang had entered the cabin. Jessie raised her hand in greeting.

"Nice work," she called to them. They, too, had changed from their black spandex outfits into casual clothes.

"Thanks!" Andrea called. "I heard you guys had a firefight."

Jessie nodded. "Yeah, we did. But we're okay. Gotta get checked by the doc...."

"Us, too. We'll be standing in line," Andrea said, laughing.

Jessie recognized the laugh as a means to get rid of tension. Right now, she felt a little giddy herself. Silly, in fact. Recognizing the symptoms from coming down off other dangerous adrenaline highs, she followed Karen to the forward cabin, where a woman in her fifties stood. She, too, wore the standard black slacks and white blouse, but a stethoscope hung from her neck. Her silvery blond hair was a mass of ringlets, and she peered through the dark-rimmed glasses perched on her nose. "Jessie?" she said with a smile. "I'm Gail Carswell. Welcome aboard. We're glad you made it here safe and sound."

Karen said, "I'll leave you two…. Jessie, when you're done, just make yourself at home. There're all kinds of drinks at the kitchen. Help yourself."

"Sure. Thanks…." She turned back to the doctor, a tall, big-boned woman with a square face and piercing gray eyes.

"Have a seat, Jessie. Let me take your blood pressure."

Jessie laughed as she sat down on a stool. "Oh, I'm sure it's shooting to the sky right now."

Gail placed the blood pressure cuff around her arm. "Rightfully so," she said, peering into her face. "Any injuries to report?"

As Gail pumped up the cuff, Jessie pointed to her chest. "Yeah, I took a bullet in my Kevlar, right here. Smarts like hell, but I'm okay."

"Hmm, we'll take a look at it in a minute." She watched the needle on the instrument. Giving her a quick smile, she murmured, "BP is good."

"That's a surprise."

Chuckling, Gail set the cuff and stethoscope aside. She pulled the curtains closed on both ends of her small office and asked Jessie to disrobe. As she did so, Jessie saw a violet-and-blue contusion on her chest.

"You got hit at close range, didn't you?" the doctor observed, running her fingers gently around the edges of the affected area.

"You can tell?"

"Yup."

"Yeah, I did. Maybe ten feet."

"I'd say the Kevlar did its job. You have a huge bruise and a lot of swelling. The skin's not broken…" she doused a cotton swab with iodine and wiped the area "…but we'll make sure no infection sets in, just in case. Otherwise, you are going to be fine, just very, very sore for a good two weeks." She dropped the swab into a can and picked up a small mirror. "Take a look. It's a beauty."

Jessie studied the reflection of her wound, turning the mirror this way and that. "Wow, that thing is red, black, blue and ugly looking. No wonder it burns."

Gail spread some ointment over the tender area. "I'm using arnica ointment here—the best thing for healing. I'll give you the tube. Apply it twice a day and make sure you never put it on broken skin. You'll be very sorry if you do—it'll sting like hell. It will also cause an infection."

The doctor's touch was gentle, almost like a butterfly. "I'm good at following orders, Doc," Jessie promised.

Carswell smiled and handed her the ointment. "Get dressed. I think you'll survive. My prescription is drink plenty of fluids."

Jessie chortled as she pulled on her tank top and shrugged into her blouse. "The first thing I'm going to do is hunt through the booze on board and see if I can't find some pisco."

It was the doctor's turn to laugh. "No pisco here, Jessie. Sorry. That's a Peruvian specialty. But I know they have tequila on board. Blue agave, I think. A little shot won't hurt you."

"I like your prescription." Jessie grinned at the woman as she slid off the stool. "Thanks, Doc."

"You're welcome…."

As Jessie exited the curtained area, she spotted Mace coming on board through the rear door. "Hey!" she called, and quickly jogged down the length of the plane toward him.

Mace was clearly surprised when she laughed and threw herself into his arms. Staggering backward at the impact, he caught her against himself. And when Jessie covered his face with big, wet puppylike kisses, wrapping her arms tightly around his neck, he laughed with her.

"I like this!" he murmured, smiling down into her uplifted face.

"A helluva welcome for a helluva warrior. Welcome home, Mace!" Exuberantly, Jessie pushed up on her toes and took his mouth hotly.

Surprise turned to sheer, unexpected pleasure as her mouth, wet and assertive, moved across his. Smiling, he held Jessie close, feeling her heart beating hard in time with his. Mace didn't care who was looking. Drowning in the splendor of her unbridled joy at seeing him, he allowed his heart to open fully to her for the first time. Breaking the kiss, he grinned. "You're *my* Wild Woman…."

"Just wait until we get home, Mace. You're a marked man in my gun sights."

Chapter 18

"Congratulations, everyone." Morgan Trayhern looked from Jessie and Mace to Chuck and Andrea Jiang, and then at Mike Houston, who was proudly grinning. They'd assembled in the war room, deep in the heart of the Perseus complex in Montana. At the head of the table, Morgan leafed through the report that Mike had compiled on the mission.

"I didn't think that Medusa, our newest agency, would produce so much so soon." Morgan gave Mike a warm look of confidence. "But I was wrong." With a shake of his head, he said, "I'm not much into metaphysics or spirituality, and so when Kai Alseoun came here asking for help to get back three of her nation's totems, I thought that was out of the purview of what we did." He looked directly at Jessie. "I guess I hadn't connected the dots on metaphysics and being a warrior. But then, Japanese samurai warriors held a spiritual code and yet defended their country. Jessie, you were chosen for this mission in a dream Kai had. I find that incredible." He grinned sheepishly.

"Well, sir, if it makes you feel any better, I'm not used to getting my marching orders from a dream, either," she said, grinning back.

"I take dreams far more seriously now," Morgan said. After picking up his cup of coffee and sipping from it, he looked back at Mike. "I know these two teams are dog tired from their long flight and want to get to bed, but will you fill them in on the rest of the mission?"

Mike sat at Morgan's right. Leaning forward, he flipped open a file. "Be happy to, boss. While you were flying back from China, we got word from the FBI in Albany, New York. As you know, Marston was in U.S. air space at the time of the swap. He'd just crossed the Canadian border, and we didn't want to take any chances that he might have learned about the break-in and would try to divert the flight. The FBI ordered up two air force fighter jets to force him to land at the nearest airport, which was Albany."

"Really?" Jessie whispered. She gave Mace a startled look. He sat up attentively.

"You're telling us that Robert Marston was forced to land and the FBI now has him in custody?" he demanded.

"That's exactly what happened." Houston grinned broadly. "Of course, he's lawyered up, but that's not a problem. The prosecutor for the state of New York is working with FBI and CIA sources. We have evidence of the wire transfer for the crystals, not to mention a lot of other artifacts he's obtained illegally. Plus the paper showing Marston had bought the Eastern Cherokee Paint Clan's crystal star, which was obtained by Vicky Mabrey and her partner, is more evidence against him being part of a global ring of thieves who buy and trade stolen ceremonial objects and ancient artifacts." Opening his hands, Mike said, "So, you got the real wolf's head crystal back, Marston is now sitting in jail and the judge has denied him bail."

"Awesome!" Jessie shouted. She raised her fist in a sign of victory. "This is just awesome!"

Mace gripped her other hand. "We did it."

Jessie didn't care who was looking. It had been hell being prim and proper on the flight across the pond. Throwing her arms around Mace's neck, she hugged him fiercely. "We did do it!"

Everyone clapped. Jessie released Mace, who

was blushing furiously at her spontaneous show of affection. She didn't care. Morgan was grinning. Houston was laughing. Chuck and Andrea nodded, understanding clearly her feelings for this man who had stood at her side and willingly risked his life for her. A fierce love for him welled up through Jessie. She gave him a burning look that said, *You're mine*....

Houston cleared his throat, a smile on his face. "There's one final leg of this mission. Jessie and Mace, in two days we ask that you fly the wolf's head crystal back to the Eastern Cherokee Reservation and hand it over to Grandmother Ivy. I've called Kai and Jake, who have agreed to meet you in Asheville and drive you to the res. The Eastern Cherokee are planning a nationwide celebration for the return of this last totem and we think that you two should share in the festivities."

"Oh, I'd love to do that!" Jessie cried.

"Me, too," Mace said, giving her a warm look. How badly he wanted to make love with her. He could see in her eyes, in the way she looked at him, that she felt the same way. It had been hell on the flight home. Even though they'd sat together, slept in their respective chairs, it wasn't close enough for him.

Morgan rose to his feet. He walked around the table and shook hands with Chuck and Andrea, thanking them for their part in making the mission a success. Jessie stood as Morgan offered his large, square hand.

"Thank you, sir, for backing this effort. I know how important restoring a nation's sacred items is to them. These artifacts are their heart and soul."

"Yes, that's what I'm learning," Morgan murmured, smiling down at her. "And thank you for putting your life on the line. I'm just glad you're back here with us, Jessie."

"You're welcome, sir." She stepped aside as Mace rose to shake Trayhern's hand.

"And, Mace," Morgan said, his voice growing serious, "I'm so impressed with you and your skills that I've asked Mike to offer you a job with us. We need top-notch linguists and excellent field agents like you. When you leave North Carolina, we'd like you to return here and talk more with us if you're interested."

Surprised and flattered, Mace said, "Thank you, sir. This is an honor...." And it was. Still, he wondered about Jessie. She was in the U.S. Army, signed on for a six-year term with one more year to go. He needed to talk with her about a lot of things, unsure if their future was going to be together or apart. "I will think about it," he promised Morgan.

Jessie smiled softly as Mace ambled into the bedroom. The sun was shining brightly through the tall windows of the third-floor condo. "Nice joint, isn't it? Sure beats the hell outta my barracks cubical in Peru." She chuckled.

Mace looked around the room. What he liked most was Jessie sitting on the edge of the bed—*their* bed. "Yeah, this is a nice place."

"Morgan takes care of his people," Jessie murmured, patting the mattress next to her. When Mace halted a foot away, she gazed up into his narrowed, dark green eyes.

"And I want to take care of you, Jessica Merrill."

The words were sweet. Unexpected. "Then come and take care of me...." As tired as she was, Jessie wanted him. Reaching out, she slid her hand into his and pulled him forward. She lay back on the soft, burgundy velvet quilt as Mace levered himself over her, propping his weight on his arms. He sent her a slow, heated smile that went straight to her core and made her ache for completion with him.

"Ever since I met you, I've wanted to love you," she told him huskily. She could feel his heat, his masculinity. What she wanted was Mace pressed on top of her, so she could feel his strength, his weight against her.

"Come here." She pushed his right shoulder so that he tipped onto the mattress beside her. With a laugh, Jessie shifted to the edge of the bed to remove his shoes, then threw them on the pale pink carpet.

"To hell with formality," she told him. "I really want you—all of you, Mace. Now…"

He allowed her to strip off his white polo shirt and tan chinos. When her fingers slid downward to pull off his boxer shorts, he felt heat bolt through him. Oh, she knew what she was doing, all right. The look in her wide blue eyes as she leaned over him, inspecting him, gleamed with a special kind of hunger. The same kind eating at him.

"All's fair in love and war, Jessie…." He pulled her down beside him.

Mace absorbed her lilting laugh as he peeled the mint-colored tank top over her head to reveal the silken, cream camisole beneath. Seeing the roundness of her breasts, the nipples puckered against the fabric, he gently cupped them. But he sobered when he saw the huge, swollen bruise on her upper chest, a reminder of the bullet that had smashed into her Kevlar vest. Mace understood the violence of the hit she'd taken, and wanted to replace pain with pleasure. As he settled his lips on the peak of her right breast and suckled her, he heard Jessie cry out. Instantly, she curled around him, her legs entangled with his, her hands reaching, nails digging into his shoulders.

Life and death. My God, they were so close to one another. Mace knew that, and as he lifted his mouth from Jessie's nipple and pulled the camisole away

from her body, the fact was even more indelibly
stamped upon his heart and soul. He moved his hand
down to unsnap her jeans, and she pushed upward.
The moment her warm breasts pressed against his
chest, he nearly lost it. And when she nibbled on his
ear and then moved her tongue sinuously down his
neck, Mace had to fight to breathe. Thinking became nearly impossible as he tugged her jeans from
her legs, then moved his hand up the firm curve of
her thigh to the creamy silk boxer shorts she wore.

Jessie lived life fully. She was such a symbol of
it! As her mouth hungrily found his, her tongue
sweeping his lower lip, he groaned and closed his
eyes. Breathing hoarsely, he kissed her back. Hard.
Moving his hand down from her waist, across the
flare of her hip, he finally divested her of the linge-
rie. Free! Naked and free at last! Mace felt her
strong, lean legs curl around him.

"You're mine!" she whispered wickedly as they
rolled over on the bed, so he was on top of her. "All
mine!" She thrust her hips upward, her legs curving
around his thighs. He was going to find out that his
Wild Woman was very real. She *was* wild. But then,
as Mace smiled down at her, his green eyes glitter-
ing with a burning need, she realized that he was a
wild man himself. Mace just hadn't shown this spontaneous side until now.

Jessie laughed with delight as he gripped her by

her hips and rolled over on his back, shifting her above him. Oh, it was so easy to straddle him, as if riding a wild stallion. Without hesitation, she brought his hardness deep into her own quivering body. The pleasure was incredible, like a bolt of white-hot lightning rippling powerfully up through her, and she gasped, her hands gripping his powerful shoulders. He held her in position, hands on her hips, grinding her against him.

Each time he groaned, she absorbed the sound like a drum echoing through her. With each lightninglike stroke, she cried out. The pleasure was increasing, to the point where she felt her entire being beginning to tremble. Mace was a part of her, she a part of him. How long had she waited for him to complete her? Complement her? Jessie had never thought she'd find a man who could meet her like this, celebrate her wildness, her womanliness. But Mace was doing exactly that. He met her ravenous sexual hunger.

Soaring with the deepening stroking motion, Jessie felt an incredible tightness gather within her. Her spine arching, she threw back her head and allowed a primal sound to rip from her throat as she was suffused with pleasure—an ecstasy that exploded through her like lava from a volcano. And Mace knew how to prolong her pleasure, to stretch out that precious, priceless moment. Then he groaned and gripped her hips hard. She knew he was releasing his life within her, and that added to her own joy. Locked together in bliss, they gave one another a gift that was as ancient as the human race.

Jessie knew that.

So did Mace.

She fell weakly against him, her head resting next to his, her body trembling and wet with perspiration. Her breath came in heaving gulps. So did his. When she felt Mace's hands move gently from her hips upward, across her damp back to stroke her shoulders, she smiled.

It was simply beyond her to move. Her heart was wide open with love for this man. All she wanted was to hear his raspy breath in time with her own, to feel his hands worshiping her body, his mouth pressed against her cheek, their bodies entwined in every possible way.

Forcing herself to move, she propped her elbows on Mace's massive, darkly-haired chest and smiled down at him. "You are a piece of work, dude."

It made Mace feel so powerful to know that he'd pleased her. Lifting his hand, he touched her tousled blond hair with his fingers. "Wild Woman. Child of nature. Lover of life."

"Yes… You got it…." She leaned down and pressed her lips against his. When she slowly moved her hips, he groaned with the pleasure of being within her.

"Life doesn't get any better than this…." He framed her face with his hands and gazed into her eyes. "You gave me so much, Jessie. You gave me hope to live again. I realize now I wasn't living at all. I needed you to show me that." He smiled. "You aren't afraid to live."

Shaking her head, she said, "No…not ever. I was taught to live life, grab it, run with it, Mace. Besides, I don't like the alternative." She turned her head and kissed the palm of his hand. Returning her gaze to his, she whispered, "And I want to run with life, live life with you in it, Mace. Now, I don't know exactly how we can do that, but that's what I want." She slid her fingers down his damp cheek. "What do you want?"

"The same thing, Jessie. Nothing less than that."

"That's good to know…." Moving her hips suggestively, she grinned. Mace groaned with pleasure.

"Listen, we're so tired we're rummy…."

"I know…but making love with you has woken me up."

Laughing softly, Mace eased her off so that she was facing him. He held her close to him as she laid her head on his arm. "Making love to you is a dream I never thought would come true," he admitted huskily against her ear.

Sliding her arm around his waist, hand splayed against his lower back, she whispered, "I know…."

"Women always know…."

"That's right, we do." She gazed at him. "Pull that spread across us? I want to sleep with you. I want to be next to you. I want to feel your heartbeat against mine…."

Mace picked up the spread and pulled it across them. Jessie snuggled into his arms and he felt her give a long, trembling sigh. As Mace closed his eyes, he knew he held such a vibrant, bold woman. Jessie truly did symbolize life as he'd never known it. But he wasn't afraid to love Jessie or walk at her side to explore it, either.

Sunlight poured through the sheer curtains as he lay there with the woman he loved in his arms. He wasn't sure what life would bring them when they woke up. Oh, he knew they would deliver the wolf's head crystal, but beyond that, it was a huge question mark. Could he stand a year's separation from Jessie as she returned to Peru? That seemed like such a cruel punishment, when he had just found her. She made him want to grasp life by the tail and live it fully, wildly. His mind spongy from the exhausting twenty-one-hour flight, he gave up on finding any answers.

Right now, the perfume of her hair, the fragrance of her as a woman filled his nostrils and he breathed it deeply into his body. She was scintillating sunlight dancing on the surface of his life. She was the wind forming into a tornado to wreak havoc wherever she landed. A softened smile touched his mouth as he felt the wings of sleep pulling him ever deeper into that dark abyss and spiral. Somehow, Mace knew that the answers would come with time. Right now, this moment, he had the woman he loved in his arms and there wasn't anything better than that.

Chapter 19

"I can hardly wait to see Grandma Ivy's face when you hand her the wolf's head totem," Jessie told Kai Alseoun, who sat in the front passenger seat beside Jake Stands Alone Carter. Kai and Jake had picked them up at the Asheville airport earlier, and now they were driving the distance to Grandma Ivy's house.

Laughing, Kai said, "She is so happy."

The day was sunny, the sky blue. Clothed in green, the Great Smoky Mountains rose in dramatic splendor above the valley of the Cherokee people. Looking around, Mace observed that the Eastern

Cherokee Reservation was clean and neat. The late-morning traffic on the two-lane asphalt road was relatively light, mostly pickups. Jake signaled a left turn, and a road of reddish, hard packed dirt stretched before them. They were heading deeper into the mountains. Mace thought the area was gorgeous. And so was Jessie.

Jessie… His heart gave a staccato beat of joy. Their two days together at the condo in Phillipsburg had been unbelievable. Mace had never wanted to make love to a woman as often as he had with Jessie. Maybe it was her innate passion for life, her enjoyment of her sexuality—and his. He felt her slide her hand across his jean-clad thigh and, turning his head, he smiled at her. Her blond hair was windblown, beautifully mussed with that red streak of fire curving across her forehead. She was his Wild Woman. Once again, his body hardened, as he saw that glimmer in her dancing blue eyes. Mace swore she could read his mind. Or maybe, as she'd said, men were easy to read, anyway.

Tonight, they would stay just outside the res at the Great Blue Heron Hotel. Tomorrow, Grandmother Ivy and the Cherokee nation would welcome back all three totems in a special ceremony led by the elders. It would be a holiday akin to Christmas, according to Kai, who'd been born and raised here.

"Now," Kai said, pointing ahead, "it's another

thirty minutes down this road before it forks. We'll go left at the junction."

"Then how far?" Mace asked.

"Another fifteen minutes. Grams lives on the side of one of the mountains. Over there, Mace."

He followed her pointing finger with his gaze. "She lives a long way from civilization."

Chuckling, Jessie said, "What Indian doesn't? We like wide-open spaces. Right, guys?"

There was a chorus of agreement from the front seat.

"No city slickers in this bunch," Mace teased, laughing.

"Jessie, have you felt the energy from the wolf's head totem?" Kai asked her.

Jessie leaned forward in her seat. She couldn't help but notice the beautiful emerald engagement ring on Kai's left hand. At the airport, Jessie could tell right away that Kai was dying to share something with them. She'd thought it had to do with the totem or the celebration, but found out that Kai and Jake had recently become engaged. The wedding was set to take place on the reservation a year from now. Jessie was so happy for Kai, who'd had a rough streak of bad luck of late. That seemed all in the past now. Jessie could see the love Kai and Jake shared every time they looked at each other. Or touched hands. Or smiled at one another.

"Briefly," Jessie answered. "But it was enough to sense its amazing power."

"Yes," Kai said. "We're fortunate to have it back where it belongs."

Jessie belonged to Mace. In the two days they spent together in the condo, she had seen her life miraculously change before her eyes—for the better. Because of him. He was a brave man in so many ways that counted with her. He tried to talk with her, share his feelings. Oh, he bumbled at times, but she dearly loved him for trying. Jessie knew it was love. She didn't know how, having never fallen in love before, but she just knew, and that was good enough for her.

Two days. Only two days. Her body still glowed from Mace's kisses, his hands exploring her and cherishing her. Then there were the little things that warmed her heart.

When she'd awakened that first morning and found the bed empty, she'd felt as if half of her was missing. It had been a terrible feeling. Jessie remembered stumbling out of bed, putting on her lavender robe and heading out the bedroom door. They'd nearly run into each other in the hall. Mace had made her breakfast and was bringing it to her as a surprise.

The gesture was so thoughtful that Jessie had been nearly overwhelmed by it all. They'd lain on the bed side by side, nibbling strawberries and sweet dairy cream, feeding each other and then stealing a kiss between bites. Oh, yeah, that was the way to wake up in the morning!

Smiling at the memory, Jessie moved her fingers along Mace's hard thigh. She saw him glance at her briefly, and the corner of his mouth quirked. If they were alone, she'd let her fingers range a lot closer to his crotch, but now was not the time to tease him. Still, she'd seen the response in his eyes and it made her feel her power as a woman, equal to the man she loved.

How could love happen so fast? Jessie wasn't sure. She thought about her friends. Kai and Jake had been childhood sweethearts, torn apart because of life situations out of their control. When they finally met again, Jake said, it was love at first sight. That he'd never stopped loving Kai even when he'd left the reservation without her as a child.

And what about Snake? Griff Hutchinson had been her nemesis in flight school and she'd hated him. Then they'd been thrown together during their mission to find the second totem. Snake, somehow, had fallen in love with a guy she'd detested! That didn't make any sense to Jessie, but her best friend's turnaround made her believe that love could develop like a thunderstorm out of the blue. Of course, she gave Kai and Snake credit. They were taking their time before they committed to marriage, which she thought was a good idea. Time revealed everyone's true colors, as her mother had told her a long time ago.

Where did that leave her and Mace? Looking at him through lowered lashes, Jessie felt her heart wrench with deep sadness. After just three days on the res, she was supposed to head back to BJS and resume her duties as a combat pilot. Jessie had been denied the thirty days' leave she'd asked for. Ordinarily, she'd barely be able to wait to harness up in the Apache helicopter. Right now, that seemed like a past life to her. And not one that she was excited to get back to.

What did excite her was Mace. They had spent so many hours talking, sharing, exploring their pasts with each other. Their two glorious days making love had flown by. Jessie wanted more quality time with him. She liked the man she was discovering beneath the CIA agent veneer. And she knew Mace liked what he saw in her, too.

"Here's our turn," Kai said as the road before them branched in a Y. Jake steered the car to the left, down a rutted dirt lane lined with heavy brush. Before long, they were driving between two green mountains.

"You take this road at dusk or early in the morning," Jake told them, "and you'll see herd after herd of deer. It's beautiful."

"It is," Kai said. "When you get the early morning fog—or smoke, as we call it—the deer appear out of it like ghosts."

It was rugged country, Jessie noted, with maple, oak and beech trees blanketing the slopes. "It's beautiful no matter which way you cut it," she said aloud. "Out on our res we've got mainly wide-open spaces, flat plains and a helluva lotta cattle."

Kai leaned between the seats and smiled back at her. Her hair was plaited into two long, black braids, reminding Jessie how glad she was that she no longer had to wear that dreadful, itchy wig!

"Flat land, *rattlesnakes* and cattle," Kai said to her with a chuckle.

"That's right," Jessie declared, holding up her hands and laughing. "And I'm not so sure that the cattle outnumber the rattlers!"

"Hang on," Jake said suddenly. "I've got a redneck in a black truck charging up on us like a bull in a china shop...."

Jessie twisted around, straining against her seat belt to catch a glimpse. Jake sounded concerned. The gravel road was wide enough for two vehicles, but a passing car could kick up stones and break a windshield. Good drivers didn't do what the driver of this truck was doing.

Jessie was glad that the wolf's head totem was safely stored in a small box in the trunk of the car.

Kai had had the good sense to strap it in the corner so it couldn't move or be tossed about.

"Hang on...here he comes," Mace warned grimly.

Jessie turned and watched the Dodge Ram roar up beside them. Frowning, she saw that the windows were tinted black, and they couldn't see who was driving. As the truck surged ahead, Jessie screamed, "Look out!" Two men with submachine guns were crouched in the rear of the pickup, their weapons pointed right at them!

Bullets shattered the side windows.

Jake slammed on the brakes as glass showered all around them.

Jessie cursed. "We've been set up by Marston!" She quickly pulled out the pistol she carried in her purse. She saw Mace reaching down to grab the weapon he carried on the side of his calf, beneath his pant leg. Up ahead, the black truck skidded to a halt. It was now backing up rapidly, straight toward them! The two men in the back started firing once more!

Ducking down, Jessie felt Jake jam the car into reverse. The windshield shattered next. Again glass shards exploded inward.

"Stop!" she yelled. "Let us take a shot at them!" Jessie knew that she and Mace were the only ones with pistols. Kai and Jake were defenseless.

Jessie jerked open the door and tumbled out into

the bushes. Scrambling to her knees, she threw herself against the side of the car and aimed at the two gunmen. Bullets shrieked and screamed around her. Some struck the hood, some flew through the vehicle. She fired again, and one man jerked backward, the submachine gun he held spinning into the air.

Hissing a curse, Jessie took careful aim at the second dude. She only had nine bullets. Each one had to count. *Aim. Squeeze. Shoot.* Eyes slitted, she targeted the bastard in the chest. He saw her and swung the barrel of his gun toward her. Jessie got off the first shot—the one that counted.

Mace tumbled out of the car and quickly crouched next to Jessie. Blood was running across his face where glass had cut his brow.

"Aim for their tires!" Jessie yelled. She stood up and, gripping her pistol with both hands, aimed at the huge, spinning wheels.

The Dodge Ram skidded to a halt. The driver tried to get the truck into gear to make an escape. Too late!

With deep satisfaction Jessie saw that her last two bullets had blown out both rear tires on the Dodge. They exploded loudly, sending rubber flying in all directions.

Firing repeatedly beside her, Mace put bullets into the rear window, which shattered. Then he aimed for the front tires.

Rage tunneled through Jessie. The truck was trying to speed away! She saw one submachine gun lying in the road. If she could put bullets into the engine, that would stop them! Running hard, toes digging into the ground, she raced for the gun.

The Dodge driver hit the accelerator just as she scooped up the weapon. The truck roared and skidded, careening wildly because three of its tires were shot out.

"No, you don't!" Jessie yelled. Seeing the pickup slide sideways, she held the submachine gun at her side and, aiming at the engine, pulled the trigger.

She'd never seen what bullets could do to a truck engine, but it was impressive. She walked the line of fire right up to the driver's door, then moved it slightly to the left and watched the bullets scream into the metal. Seconds later, there was a huge explosion.

The blast knocked Jessie off her feet and wrenched the submachine gun out of her hand. The black truck flew upward, landing a hundred feet away, in the bushes near the foot of the mountain. Rolling over and over, Jessie felt the heat from the blast. Shakily getting up on her knees seconds later, she saw two men leap from the cab and start running up the slope.

No way! Looking up, she saw Mace barreling

down the road toward her. She saw fear for her safety in his eyes, but rage, too. Looking beyond him, she saw Kai and Jake emerging from the ruined car. They appeared to be uninjured.

"Here, Jessie!" Mace threw her another ammunition clip for her weapon.

Catching it midair, Jessie took the pistol that Mace passed to her.

"We're going to catch those bastards!" she hissed, running into the woods, Mace right beside her. She watched as their attackers split up and disappeared into the trees.

"I'll take the one with the red baseball cap," he yelled.

"I'll take the dude with the blue cap!"

"Kai's calling 911 on her cell phone," Mace cried as he peeled off to the right.

"Okay! Be careful!"

"You, too!"

Breathing hard, her teeth gritted, Jessie followed the would-be assassin into the forest. The smooth-barked, gray beech trees were huge, the oaks smaller, their bark rough and dark brown in comparison. The ground was softer here. There wasn't much undergrowth, but the leaves were damp and some of them slippery from an earlier rain. Holding up her pistol, Jessie jammed the cartridge into the butt. Running uphill, dodging between trees, she cocked the weapon.

Up the steep slope ahead of her, Jessie could see the man's back. He was a big dude with broad shoulders. Whoever he was, he was damn agile and fast! Well, so was she! All those years of working out and running were going to count for something now!

Jessie got within a hundred feet of the fleeing assassin. She was unable to take a shot because the trees grew so close together that she'd waste bullets trying to wing the son of a bitch. No, she had good wind. Her legs felt strong. She was going to have to wait until he either got tired or made a mistake. Either one was okay with her.

In the distance, to her right, she heard a spate of gunfire. Mace! Had he found the enemy? Killed him? Or was he being fired on? The terror that sizzled through Jessie made her slow down. Maybe it wasn't such a good idea that they'd split up. But in the heat of the attack, it had seemed logical for each of them to go after their enemy.

Fear stabbed her wildly pounding heart. Was Mace okay? Was he lying bleeding somewhere? Dead? *Oh, no!*

Air rasped from her open mouth as she ran up the slope. The man in the blue cap reached an outcropping of rock, where he turned toward her, a smirk on his face. He raised his weapon.

With a grunt, Jessie threw herself to the ground. The man's face was fully visible now. He was white, not Native American. And he had a pistol aimed directly at her. *Damn!*

There was no place to hide. Raising her own pistol, she felt a bullet whiz by her ear. Too close! Gasping, she steadied her weapon. *Don't be in a hurry.* She only had nine bullets. Each one had to count.

A second bullet dug up dirt right in front of her face. Out of instinct, Jessie jerked back on the trigger. The pistol bucked in her hand. *Damn!* Momentarily blinded, she rolled to the left and kept moving until she reached the cover of a wide gray beech. A third bullet smashed into the trunk of the tree, no more than a foot from where she crouched behind it.

Gasping, Jessie wiped the dirt off her face. Her vision was blurred. Tears ran freely down her cheeks. The bastard knew what to do: blind her so she couldn't draw a bead on him. This was a professional.

Her heart slammed into her ribs. Oh, how she wished for an Apache helicopter right now! The slim pistol she gripped seemed so powerless, so effeminate, so useless.

Jessie waited. The gunshots stopped. Taking a chance, she quickly peeked from behind the tree. Blue cap was gone from the outcropping! Lurching forward, she started on up the hill. Within a minute, she'd crested the limestone formation. From the top, she saw the man fleeing down a small slope. He was within range and there were no trees nearby to protect him.

Sinking down on one knee, holding the pistol in both hands, Jessie tried to control her breathing enough to draw an accurate bead. She aimed for the bastard's back and fired. Once. Twice. Three times.

The man shrieked.

Jessie leaped to her feet. She watched with grim satisfaction as one of her bullets found his leg and he buckled over. Instantly, he was thrown forward, the force knocking him to the ground. Jessie watched as the pistol he carried flew a good thirty feet away from him.

Without hesitating, she ran down the slope after him, watching him roll over and grab his lower leg. Blood was pouring from his calf.

Skidding to a halt twenty feet from him, Jessie snarled, "Roll over on your belly and put your hands out in front of you. *Now!*"

He glared at her, gripping his leg. "You bitch! You shot me!"

"No shit! I'll do it again. Roll over, or do you want a hole in the other leg? Then you'd have a matched pair. Go on, make my day, you bastard...."

Cursing, he let go of his bloody leg. Giving her one last glare, he slowly rolled onto his stomach.

Jessie wanted his pistol. As he stretched his arms

over his head, she moved forward quickly to pick it up. As she leaned down, keeping her gun trained on the would-be assassin, she heard someone approaching from below. She refused to take her eyes off the man. Fumbling around with her hand, she finally located his weapon. Gripping it, she stood up and backed off as Kai ran up the slope toward her.

"He's down and wounded," Jessie called.

"Dead, I hope," Kai yelled angrily as she covered the last hundred feet to where Jessie stood.

Shaking her head, Jessie said, "No. I just winged the bastard. You know who they are?"

"I haven't a clue. We got the sheriff's department and the Cherokee police on the way." Kai leaned down, hands on her knees, breathing hard. "What a helluva surprise."

"What about Mace? Have you heard from him? Is Jake with him?"

Straightening, Kai pulled a cell phone from her pocket. "Yeah, he's fine. He took that other dude down fast. Jake is with him and called from his cell. I'd hoped to find you, cut off this guy's escape. You okay?"

"Yeah, just pissed off is all. You two okay?"

Looking at her arm, Kai shrugged. "A lot of flying glass hit us. We both look like pincushions."

"We're not as bad off as he is," Jessie said, a dark grin curving her lips as she watched their unhappy captive. Her heart, however, turned to Mace. She loved that man. And now, maybe this mission was really over and she could set her sights on him. On them and their future together.

Chapter 20

"I've had enough excitement for one day," Jessie wearily confided to Mace as he emerged from the bathroom at the Great Blue Heron Hotel, a turquoise towel wrapped around his waist. It was nearly 2200—10:00 p.m.—and she was whipped.

Rubbing another towel across his wet hair, he smiled. "Makes two of us, I think."

Jessie had been peppered with glass across her upper body. She was more fortunate than he in that he'd had to go to the local hospital and have glass removed from his forehead. None of the shards had hit her in the face, thank goodness.

Now, she sat exhausted on the bed, dressed in her lavender silk nightgown, her slim legs dangling over the edge. She was beautiful no matter what she wore—or didn't wear.

Dropping the towel, Mace sat next to her and pulled her close. Jessie sighed and curved against him, her head on his shoulder, her arm wrapped around his waist. "This is what we needed and didn't get all day." He closed his eyes and inhaled the fragrance of her hair and skin.

"Agreed." Jessie closed her eyes, content to feel Mace's warm flesh beneath her cheek. She loved his ability to share, to know she needed to be held right now without her having to say so. "I'm glad Grandma Ivy got the wolf's head totem back, though."

Chuckling, Mace said, "Yeah, I was a little worried about that. I saw some bullet holes in the trunk of the car when we brought that one dude back down off the mountain. I was really scared one of those bullets might have hit it, but it was safe."

"Just seeing Grams take charge of that last totem made my day," Jessie said softly. She moved her fingers across his lower arm, trying to imprint the feel of him. Her heart ached, because shortly, she'd have to leave him. And she didn't want to. It was the last thing in the world she wanted right now.

"Well, we'll get to see her again at the ceremony

tomorrow. I'm glad Grams is going to honor Kai. After all the hell she went through, being congratulated by the entire Cherokee nation should help restore the respect she thought she'd lost with her people."

"Kai's a heroine," Jessie said. "And everywhere we went on the res yesterday after that little tango with the bad guys, you could hear people talking about her in glowing terms. I think this ceremony will heal her a great deal."

Nodding, Mace murmured, "I know. Oh, I talked to Mike Houston about the man our gun-toting friends said hired them for the hit on us. He said Kyle Pierce probably has a link to Robert Marston. Right now he's trying to find that connection. He's in jail and going nowhere."

"I think Marston made a phone call," Jessie said. "And knowing him like we do now, it's clear he never gets directly implicated in any of his dirty work. He goes through three or four people to get the order taken care of the way he wants."

"Yeah, for an eighty-year-old dude, he's smart like a fox. But we knew that. Anyway, Mike's tracking it down, but we both feel there's a missing link, that Pierce might be connected to Marston through another man, yet unknown. I think over time he'll fess up, because the prosecutor is waving a deal under his nose."

"Less time in prison?" Jessie growled.

"Yes. But if it will lead us to Marston, it's worth it, don't you think?"

"I do. I just hope that the U.S. State Department can work with the Chinese government to return all those pipes and other ceremonial items to the appropriate nations."

"Mike said he's working on that angle, too. Actually, Morgan Trayhern is. He's got contacts in the State Department and he now understands, as never before, what Indian ceremonial items mean to a nation and its people." He smiled. "I think Annie Dazen, Jason's wife, has educated him on that point."

"That's good," Jessie said. "The world is made up of many interesting realities, not just one person's reality. I'll give Morgan credit. He's changing and opening up his perspective. That can do nothing but good for everyone."

Mace nodded. "The New York prosecutor is going to take his time in tracking down all of Marston's illegal activities. The Canadian government is working with us, too, and that's good news."

"I didn't know that." Jessie perked up. "That's great!"

"Plus, as if that isn't enough good news," Mace said, smiling, "Kai's engagement to Jake will become official tomorrow, shortly after the totem ceremony."

"They've earned their happiness with one another."

Mace turned and pressed a soft kiss to Jessie's damp, recently washed hair. "So have we…"

Easing her head back so she could look up into his green eyes, which were tender with love, Jessie heaved a painful sigh. "I thought we had, but that's not how it's going to work out, Mace."

"What do you mean?"

"Three days from now, my temporary duty ends. I'm due back at BJS in Peru. You aren't going with me, Mace, and that pisses me off. I finally find a man that I'm endlessly fascinated with, who's a wonderful lover and someone I can confide in like a best friend, and suddenly you're gone." She snapped her fingers. "Just like that."

"When we were at the sheriff's office earlier, didn't you wonder where I went after we booked those dudes who shot at us?"

Thinking back, Jessie said, "Yeah…I guess I did, but I was still so pumped up on adrenaline that I didn't give it much thought. I knew you wanted to talk to Houston."

Mace looked so damn inviting sitting there with a towel draped over his hips. If she wasn't so exhausted, Jessie would peel it off him, no questions.

She saw the merriment in his eyes. "What's going on? You look like the cat that ate the poor canary. What do you know that I don't, Mace?"

He smiled innocently. Squeezing her fingers gently, he said, "What would you do if I told you that I'll be sharing that flight to Lima with you?"

Jessie thought she'd heard wrong. But when she saw Mace's smile widen, she whispered, "Are you *serious?*"

Taking her hand, he kissed the back of it gently, then said, "I called my CIA handler. I suggested that more investigation needed to be done in Lima on the antique and grave-site thefts concerning the heist of the seven-pointed crystal star. I convinced him to let me continue to compile a list of people who worked either directly for Marston or through other operatives we already know about because of Snake's discoveries in Lima."

"That means…" Jessie paused, her eyes widening "…that you'll be in Lima?" The Peruvian capital was a couple hours from where her black ops was located, but so what? It was an easy flight from Cuzco down to Lima. Excited, she gripped his hand in hers. "Mace, how long? How long will you be there?"

"As long as it takes," he murmured. "I've already received a list of potential suspects and antique dealers. Not only that, but we'll be working with a special, newly created archeology theft bureau within the Peruvian government, with a staff who can't be bought off with bribes. So I'll be down there for quite a while helping to set this up, as well as interfacing with them as the official liaison of the U.S. government on this new agenda. We're going to find out who the thieves are and we're going to stop them."

"Peru deserves to preserve her history, not have it stolen and sold worldwide. Bringing Marston to justice is going to be like firing a cannon across the bow of those rich collectors who think they're impervious to law enforcement in any country."

She saw the hard glint in his eyes. Moving her palm to his cheek, she said, "This is the greatest news, Mace! We'll be able to see each other at least once a week."

He pressed his hand against hers. "I know you have a year left on your present assignment. After that you can decide whether to reenlist or quit the army and take a civilian job."

"Does the CIA have any openings for an ex-Apache combat pilot?"

Grasping her hand, he held it between his. "I did a little research on that possibility. My handler says that there's a CIA contingent at the Lima airport. They're disguised as a freight company for cover. Their helo pilot is due to rotate back to the States in about a year. I figure, if all goes right, you could bid on this job as his replacement. Of course, you'd have a month of training before taking over the position. Interested?"

Was she ever! Excitedly, she said, "Dude, this is too good to be true! Yes! I want his job! Sooner rather than later!" She gave a wild whoop and threw her arms around Mace's bare shoulders as they fell back onto the bed together.

"What about Morgan Trayhern? He offered you a job at Perseus."

Shrugging, Mace murmured, "I thought about it, but I like the CIA for now. It was an honor to be asked, though. I enjoyed working with him and his people."

"I liked working with *you!*"

Laughing with her, Mace rolled her onto her back. Never mind that his towel came unhitched and fell away as he placed Jessie beneath him, careful not to put his full weight upon her. Drowning in her smile, the joy radiating from her blue eyes, Mace leaned down and kissed her. Her mouth was hot, eager and hungry. The pent-up terror of the day, the brutal possibility that they could have died out there on that dirt road, dissolved as she moved her tongue across his lower lip and then gently nipped it. Her hands roamed his torso, then spanned downward to caress his hips and naked butt. Gripping him, she thrust her pelvis upward, letting him know just how much she wanted him. Grinning against her curved lips, he whispered, "So, you like the idea of working for the CIA?"

Leaning up, she trailed a series of kisses along his earlobe, neck and jaw. "Mmm, I like the idea of being with *you,* Mace. That's all that matters to me. My life took a helluva turn when you came into it. My mother told me a long time ago never to look back, but forward."

Kissing her mouth, he eased away and trapped her beneath him. Her hair was tousled, her eyes huge and shining. "I like looking forward with you, Jessie." His smile faded. Lifting his hand, he touched the golden strands of her hair. "Are you sure about this? You've been with the BJS for four years now. That's a long time. You made a lot of friends there. What about Snake?"

"Snake and I are like sisters. It doesn't matter where we go in life, we'll always be close. Major Stevenson knows she can't keep our original team together forever. We know she's moving on and bringing fresh new pilots in so we can get on with our lives, in or out of the army."

Jessie sighed. "The Black Jaguar Squadron has served the world well, Mace. We've loved what we've been doing, and we're proud of the contributions we've made as a team of women in a man's army. But we're all tired of spending so much energy to prove ourselves. Now that the numbers show how good we are, we can ease off and get on with the rest of our lives. And I think someday we're going to look back on this time and see just how remarkable and incredible it really was."

Nodding, Mace said, "I know you're right. I've often heard veterans talk about the bonds formed with brothers in arms. They never leave you."

"Nor should they," Jessica said. "I'm sure the major will have some huge farewell party when we all move on. And I'm sure she'll keep in touch with all of us and vice versa. Women tend to do that. We don't forget and we don't leave people behind."

"One of your many good traits," Mace said seriously.

"Knowing the major, she'll probably put Snake in charge of the party." Jessie rolled her eyes. "I can see it all now—endless pisco flowing from some fountain where all you have to do is put your paper cup under it and drink until you fall down!"

"You live hard, you party hard," Mace said, laughing with her. "It's the way it is."

Sliding her hand along his cheek, she said, "And I want to live hard and party hard with you, guy."

After brushing a series of soft kisses across her brow, Mace held her warm gaze. "Forever, if you want?"

"Forever. I'm not the kind of gal who commits unless it's for the long haul."

"I kinda thought so." Mace eased off of her and dropped his towel on the floor beside the bed, leaving him standing naked. Her admiring look made him feel incredibly strong and powerful as he walked over and switched off the light. Instantly, the room was drenched in darkness. Padding back, he murmured, "Let's go to bed and plan our future, shall we?"

Jessie smiled and eased the silk nightgown from her body, letting it slide off the bed. Mace pulled the covers aside and she joined him underneath, pressing the warmth of her bare skin to his. "This is what I want, Mace. I want the time to get to know you in every possible way. I don't want to rush into anything. I think we owe ourselves this gift."

Mace closed his eyes and ran his hands up and down her arms. "I learned the value of taking my time. I was a friend to my wife for a long time before I married her." He looked at Jessie, feeling her feminine curves. "I think any good relationship starts out with a strong base of friendship. Don't you?"

She was studying him, a tender smile on her lips. "Friends and sex?"

Laughing, Mace nodded. "Yeah, why not? What we have is great." It was more than great. It was the best lovemaking Mace had ever experienced. That took nothing away from his marriage or his wife; each woman was unique, he knew. Jessica was so special, and Mace himself had grown and changed. They complemented each other beautifully, as far as he was concerned. He wanted to show her that a man could be a friend *and* a lover to her. That combination, he felt, was the right recipe for a long-term relationship that would, sooner or later, end in marriage.

Nuzzling his neck with her lips, his Wild Woman whispered, "I like what we have, Mace. And I like where we're going—together...." After a searing kiss, she added "Forever..."

* * * * *

If you enjoyed Wild Woman,
*you'll love Lindsay McKenna's
next book, ENEMY MINE,
available May 2005 from HQN Books.*

IT'S A JUNGLE OUT THERE...
AND WE'RE TURNING UP THE HEAT!

ONE WOMAN.
ONE DEADLY VIRUS.
ONE SCANDALOUS COVER-UP.

Get ready for an explosive situation
as Dr. Jane Miller races to stop a
dangerous outbreak and decide
which man to trust.

THE AMAZON STRAIN
by Katherine Garbera

May 2005

Available at your favorite local retailer.

www.SilhouetteBombshell.com

SBTAS

If you enjoyed what you just read,
then we've got an offer you can't resist!

Take 2 bestselling love stories FREE!
Plus get a FREE surprise gift!

Clip this page and mail it to Silhouette Reader Service®

IN U.S.A.
3010 Walden Ave.
P.O. Box 1867
Buffalo, N.Y. 14240-1867

IN CANADA
P.O. Box 609
Fort Erie, Ontario
L2A 5X3

YES! Please send me 2 free Silhouette Bombshell™ novels and my free surprise gift. After receiving them, if I don't wish to receive any more, I can return the shipping statement marked cancel. If I don't cancel, I will receive 4 brand-new novels every month, before they're available in stores! In the U.S.A., bill me at the bargain price of $4.69 plus 25¢ shipping & handling per book and applicable sales tax, if any*. In Canada, bill me at the bargain price of $5.24 plus 25¢ shipping & handling per book and applicable taxes**. That's the complete price and a savings of 10% off the cover prices—what a great deal! I understand that accepting the 2 free books and gift places me under no obligation ever to buy any books. I can always return a shipment and cancel at any time. Even if I never buy another book from Silhouettte, the 2 free books and gift are mine to keep forever.

200 HDN D34H
300 HDN D34J

Name	(PLEASE PRINT)	
Address	Apt.#	
City	State/Prov.	Zip/Postal Code

Not valid to current Silhouette Bombshell™ subscribers.

Want to try another series?
Call 1-800-873-8635 or visit www.morefreebooks.com.

* Terms and prices subject to change without notice. Sales tax applicable in N.Y.
** Canadian residents will be charged applicable provincial taxes and GST.
  All orders subject to approval. Offer limited to one per household.
  ® and ™ are registered trademarks owned and used by the trademark owner and
  or its licensee.

BOMB04   ©2004 Harlequin Enterprises Limited

eHARLEQUIN.com

The Ultimate Destination for Women's Fiction

For **FREE online reading**, visit
www.eHarlequin.com now and enjoy:

Online Reads
Read **Daily** and **Weekly** chapters from
our Internet-exclusive stories by your
favorite authors.

Interactive Novels
Cast your vote to help decide how these
stories unfold...then stay tuned!

Quick Reads
For shorter romantic reads, try our
collection of Poems, Toasts, & More!

Online Read Library
Miss one of our online reads?
Come here to catch up!

Reading Groups
Discuss, share and rave with other
community members!

For great reading online,
visit www.eHarlequin.com today!

INTONL04R